TAMING A SEA-HORSE

Books by Robert B. Parker

TAMING A SEA-HORSE
A CATSKILL EAGLE
VALEDICTION
LOVE AND GLORY
THE WIDENING GYRE
CEREMONY
A SAVAGE PLACE
EARLY AUTUMN
LOOKING FOR RACHEL WALLACE
WILDERNESS
THE JUDAS GOAT
THREE WEEKS IN SPRING *(with Joan Parker)*
PROMISED LAND
MORTAL STAKES
GOD SAVE THE CHILD
THE GODWULF MANUSCRIPT

A SPENSER NOVEL

Robert B. Parker

Taming a Sea-Horse

Delacorte Press/Seymour Lawrence

Published by
Delacorte Press/Seymour Lawrence
1 Dag Hammarskjold Plaza
New York, N.Y. 10017

Designed by Laurence Alexander

Library of Congress Cataloging-in-Publication Data

Parker, Robert B., 1932–
Taming a sea-horse.

I. Title.
PS3566.A686T35 1986 813′.54
ISBN 0-385-29461-1
Library of Congress Catalog Card Number: 85-29297

MANUFACTURED IN THE UNITED STATES OF AMERICA
FIRST PRINTING

For Joan

Nay, we'll go
Together down, sir. Notice Neptune though,
Taming a sea-horse, thought a rarity,
Which Claus of Innsbruck cast in bronze for me!

Robert Browning, "My Last Duchess"

TAMING A SEA-HORSE

1

I hadn't had lunch with Patricia Utley since the last time the Red Sox won the pennant. That seems like another way to say *never*, but in fact it had been ten years. We were looking at the menu and sipping margaritas (on the rocks, salt) in a restaurant called Bogie's on West 26th Street in Manhattan.

"Veal's awfully good here," Patricia said.

"So are the margaritas," I said.

She smiled. "Margaritas are good everywhere."

Ten years had made little impression on Patricia Utley. She was still small and blond and fine-boned. She still wore big black-rimmed round glasses. She still looked very good.

The waitress came and took our order and went away. She came back shortly with a second margarita for me. Patricia Utley still had most of hers left. It's hard to make a margarita last and with each sip it becomes harder. I put my glass down, licked a little salt off my upper lip. No problem. I'd just leave it there a while and then I'd have another little sip.

"Have you found April yet?" I said.

"Steven has traced her to another call house on the West Side," she said. "Ninety-sixth and Central Park West." She gave me the address.

I turned the margarita glass slowly on the tablecloth with my right hand.

"Decent place?" I said.

"At the moment," she said. "But only at the moment. When she gets a little used up she'll be replaced and they'll turn her out into something a little less plush."

"And when she gets used up there?" I said.

Patricia Utley nodded. "To something still less plush."

I drank some of my margarita.

"Down and down I go," I said. "Round and round I go."

"She'll be in a spin," Patricia Utley said. "But she won't be enjoying it."

I had taken a bit larger sip than I'd intended. The margarita was gone. Probably if I had another one, I'd be able to think just what I should do about April Kyle. I nodded at the waitress. She brought me a new drink and one for Patricia Utley.

"Maybe I can talk with her a bit," I said.

Patricia nodded. "It might help. Steven talked with

her but it did no good. Whether she'll respond to you I don't know. You sent her to me."

"I know," I said. "Seemed like a good idea at the time."

"I think it was. We made real progress with her. She had learned how to behave, maybe even had started to get some values."

"And regular medical checks. No clap, no herpes."

"There's always whores," Patricia said. "Always. And someone has always run them. That doesn't mean that some ways aren't better than others."

The waitress came with our veal.

When she went away, I said, "I know. That's why I sent her to you. She was going to be a whore, no matter what."

"And my girls get fairly paid and they are not abused and they are free to leave." She shrugged. "I never claimed it was Smith College."

"No need to be defensive," I said. "No one accused you of being Smith College."

Patricia smiled. I finished my margarita before starting the veal. Sequence is important.

"Do you have a client in this affair?" Patricia said.

"No, I'm on spec," I said.

"That was the same fee you got last time you were involved with April."

I ate some veal. "Yum yum," I said.

"Still sentimental," Patricia said. "I thought age might have toughened you up a little."

"You called me," I said.

She smiled again. "And how will you proceed?" she said. She hadn't touched her second drink.

"I'll see her, reason with her. When that doesn't work I'll improvise. You going to drink that drink?"

"No," she said. "Are you going to remind me of starving children somewhere?"

"Nope, I was going to warn you about scurvy."

She took the margarita and put it in front of me.

"Save yourself," she said.

I took a sip. It went surprisingly well with the veal. On the other hand, the fourth margarita goes surprisingly well with everything.

"She left you with no explanation," I said.

"That's right. Simply disappeared. Her room was cleaned out and she was gone. But no note, no phone call, no good-bye. When I called you I had no idea where she was."

"Why would she leave you and go to another, ah, service? Money?"

"I don't think so. I think she was seduced."

"Patricia," I said, "I don't wish to be coarse, but she's a whore. She's been a whore since she was sixteen."

"And now she's twenty," Patricia said, "and she's still a whore. But whores do what they do for a lot of reasons, and I think April is in love with somebody that has her working there."

"A pimp?"

Patricia Utley shrugged. "Sure," she said, "for lack of a better word. My guess is that he's really more of a recruiter."

"Like for G.E. or Indiana U?"

"Yes. It's done. You find that you don't have a particular kind of girl in your stable, you shop around or you get hold of someone who'll shop around, and he finds what you need: blond Miss America, exotic Latin, somebody who looks like Sophie Tucker, and he recruits her for you."

"Always *he?*"

"No, a lot of recruiting is done in lesbian bars. But in this case it's a he."

"What determines what kind of woman you want in your stable?" I said. "Customer demand?"

"Yes," Patricia said.

"Do you recruit?"

"No. I don't need to. My whores come because they've heard about my operation and because they want to work for me. Except the ones that are sent me by detectives from Boston."

The waitress cleared our dishes. We ordered cheesecake for dessert. Patricia Utley ordered coffee. Not me. No point screwing up four margaritas.

"You were the best I could do," I said. "All the other options she had were worse."

Patricia Utley smiled. "Thanks," she said.

The waitress came with the cheesecake. Mine had cherries on it. I remained calm. Normally cherry cheesecake makes my nostrils flare dramatically. I took a small, dignified bite. Control.

"Being someone's whore is not an ideal option for anyone," I said. "I notice for instance that you're not. But ideal options aren't something I have much to do with. Most of the time I'm shuttling between bad and worse."

"With me she has choice," Patricia said. "No one is coerced with me."

"At least not by you. The world probably coerces them some."

"I can't help that," Patricia Utley said.

"Me either," I said. I had another bite of cherry cheesecake.

"But you keep trying," she said.

"Else what's a heaven for," I said.

"And falling short."

I shrugged. The discussion was distracting me from the cheesecake.

"But you keep doing it," she said.

"April Kyle got a better deal out of life than she would have if I hadn't been around," I said. "I got her choices. It's the best anyone gets. It's all I'll try to give her this time. If she's where she'd rather be, then that's where she ought to be."

"Even if later on it will destroy her?"

"One day at a time," I said. My cheesecake was gone. My pulse rate slowed. Patricia Utley paid the check.

On 26th Street we walked east. It was spring in New York, and the street litter was beginning to dry in the pale sun.

"Don't underestimate the impact that her pimp has on her," Patricia Utley said.

"If she has one."

Patricia Utley looked at me almost sadly. "April has one," she said. "In spite of everything, in spite of all they know to the contrary, whores want love. It's not money that they whore for. It's love, or the hope of it."

"Why should they be different?"

"Because by the time they get to be twenty years old they have ample evidence that love is nonsense."

"Put money in thy purse?"

"That's some kind of quote," Patricia Utley said, "but I don't know from where. Yes. Of course, put money in thy purse."

"You management types are all the same," I said. "Anti-romantics."

"But the whores aren't," Patricia said. "That may be the trick of it."

"I'm not anti-romantic," I said.

"You're male," she said. "You can afford it."

"If I were female would it lead me to whoredom?"

She shook her head. "No, I don't think so."

We reached Sixth Avenue. "So it's not the whole trick."

She was looking for a cab. "Maybe not."

"Everyone wants love," I said. "Not everyone whores."

She gestured toward a cab. It zipped past us. "Shit," she said. She looked for another one. Downtown a block two guys in tan raincoats flagged the next cab. She exhaled softly and turned and looked at me. Under her careful makeup I could see lines at her mouth and eyes. Natural light is tough. "I'm not a philosopher," she said. "You don't have to know how coal was made in order to mine it. But I think April's future will be a lot brighter if you get her out of that call service, and to do that, I think you're going to have to get her away from a pimp that she thinks loves her."

"Pimps don't love anybody," I said.

"You know that. I know that. Whores don't know that."

"Did you always know that?" I said.

A cab angled across the traffic from the east side of Sixth Avenue and stopped.

"You want a ride uptown?" Patricia said.

"No, thanks," I said. "I like to walk. You going to answer my question?"

She said, "No," and got in the cab. I closed the door behind her and the cab pulled back into the traffic.

2

I went another block east to Fifth Avenue and walked slowly uptown to the St. Regis Hotel on 55th Street. I had a room there. I noticed that the glitz incidence intensifies above 49th Street and attributed that to the presence of Rockefeller Center. It was my most useful insight.

It was five o'clock when I got to my room. I turned on the TV and watched the news on WNBC. I studied the room service menu. It was too early for supper but it's important to plan ahead. At five-thirty I called April at the number Patricia Utley had given me.

A woman's voice said, "Tiger Lilies."

"April Kyle, please."

"May I say who's calling?"

"Spenser."

"Thank you, Mr. Spenser, would you hold, please?"

Some easy-listening Muzak came onto the phone. I held it away from my ear. If you listened close for long, it gave you cavities. The Muzak stopped. April's voice came on the phone.

"Spenser?"

"With an *s,*" I said. "Like the poet."

"Well . . . how are you?"

"Almost perfect," I said. "I'm in town and want to take you to dinner."

"I . . . Well, I'm working tonight. I'm . . . we're not supposed to go out on nonbusiness dates."

"How about breakfast? You allowed personal breakfasts?"

"Breakfast?"

April hadn't gotten too much smarter.

"Or brunch, or lunch, or an afternoon snack, or juice and graham crackers after recess," I said. "I'd like to see you."

"Well, breakfast, if it's not too early. I, um, I get to sleep real late usually."

"Name the time," I said.

"Well, ah, could it be, like noon?"

"Sure. I'll pick you up."

"No. No, I'll meet you."

"Okay," I said. "How about the Brasserie. You know where that is?"

"Sure. Okay. I'll meet you there at noon."

"You'll recognize me," I said. "You haven't forgotten what I look like?"

"No." She giggled. "You look like a nice thug."

"Gee," I said, "you remembered."

"Yes. See you tomorrow. Bye."

It was five-forty. Susan's last appointment was at five-ten. She wouldn't be available until after six. I watched the news some more. The longer I put off dinner, the later it would be before I had nothing to do. If I timed it right, I could call Susan and then have dinner and then be sleepy and go to bed. I read the menu again. I'd had a big lunch. It would be self-indulgent to have a big dinner. I didn't have to eat and drink to entertain myself. I could go out. New York was a spring festival of things to do. I could go down to 42nd Street and buy a nice hand-painted tie.

The five o'clock news ended. The six o'clock news began. The guys who read the news at six had deeper voices. Authoritative. If that trend continued, the guys who read the eleven o'clock news would sound like Paul Robeson.

I called Susan. Her voice came on after the second ring.

"Hello, this is Dr. Silverman. I can't answer the phone now, but if you have a message for me please leave it at the sound of the beep."

I said, "Shit." But it was before the beep, so it didn't count. After the beep I said, "Doctor, I have a problem with priapism and need an appointment with you as soon as I can get one. I'm at the St. Regis Hotel. Call me to set up a time." Then I hung up and watched the news some more. Not a hell of a lot had happened since I'd watched it before. I called room service and ordered a Cobb Salad and a couple of bottles of Heineken.

The phone rang. I answered it. Susan said, "This is Dr. Silverman. Take a cold shower and call me in the morning."

I said, "Hello, ducky. How has your day been?"

"Some of those people are crazy," she said.

"Your patients?"

"Yes."

"But you're a psychologist. Don't you sort of expect that?"

"My last appointment told me he didn't believe in psychotherapy. It makes you dependent, he says."

"So what's he going to do instead?"

"Snort cocaine, I believe."

"Oh."

"Have you found April?" Susan said.

"I talked with her on the phone, and we're having lunch, she says breakfast, tomorrow noon."

"Is she all right?"

"She sounds all right, but Patricia Utley says she's headed for trouble." I repeated my conversation with Patricia.

"And if she's not willing to leave?" Susan said.

"I could overpower her and bring her to you."

"And hold her while we did therapy?"

"Yeah."

"Even though your neck is considerably bigger than your brain," Susan said, "you probably know that you cannot do therapy with an unwilling patient."

"I was afraid you'd spoil it."

"So what will you do?" Susan said.

"Tell her what I fear, and get out of the way. She'll do what she wants to," I said.

"Or needs to," Susan said.

"Or has to."

"Which makes her like anyone else," Susan said. "When are you coming home?"

"I suppose it depends on April," I said.

"Not too much should depend on April, I think," Susan said.

"I know," I said.

"I miss you," Susan said.

"Yes," I said. "Isn't it lovely."

3

The Brasserie is on East 53rd Street, right underneath the Four Seasons, a few steps down into a low-ceilinged room with a horseshoe counter to the left and tables with red-checkered tablecloths to the right. It was kind of a semi-elegant French-flavored diner and it was always open.

I had us a table near the wall when April came in and looked around. There's a street-level landing before you come down into the room, and it presents a nearly irresistible platform. Most people posed on it when they came in. April posed a bit longer than most. She wasn't pudgy anymore. She was high-fashion thin. With very bright makeup, well applied and stark. Very current. Her hair was shoulder length. She was wearing a pink coverall with cropped pants over an aqua jersey top. There were big pink and aqua beads around her neck and matching earrings. The collar of her black tweed jacket was turned up and she was wearing pink-rimmed Elvis Costello sunglasses.

When she finished her pose, she looked at me and smiled brilliantly and came down the stairs.

I stood and she put her arms around me and kissed me on the cheek. She smelled good. She looked good. I held her chair for her. She sat.

"Oh, it's so nice to see you," April said. "What are you doing here?"

"Think about eating," I said. "Then I'll tell you."

"Oh, you order something for us," she said. Her eyes didn't settle on me or anything but moved over the crowd in the restaurant. She was like the buyer at a horse auction.

"No preference?"

She laughed. "No, I know you'll choose something good."

The waiter stopped at our table with the coffeepot. "Coffee?" he said.

April looked at me. I nodded. She smiled dazzlingly at the waiter and nodded too. He poured some for us both. I ordered eggs Benedict for April and a club sandwich for me. When the waiter left, April pressed the palms of her hands together in front of her and said, "Oh, I knew you'd order something just right."

"It's God-given," I said. "I can't really take the credit."

April widened her eyes and smiled even more brightly and nodded vigorously. She looked around the room some more. Her eyes hesitated at the counter, went on, returned to the counter, and then moved away. I shifted into a more comfortable position in my chair and looked at the counter. It was crowded. I couldn't tell who she was looking at.

"How have you been?" I said.

"Oh, it's fun," she said. "It really is. I've met so many people and I have been just everywhere. I went to Nice last year with a client."

"Ever hear from your parents?"

"No."

"You happy?"

"What's not to be happy?" she said. "I have money, I go out every night. Clothes, fun."

"You seem to have learned a lot," I said. "Very adult now. Worldly, sort of. Poised."

"Oh, thank you. Mrs. Utley helped me a lot. She helps all the girls. She really does. I . . . I'm very grateful you fixed me up with her."

Uncle Pandarus. The waiter came by and added coffee to my cup. April's was untouched.

"How is Mrs. Silverman?" April said. She leaned toward me, her hands clasped, her chin resting on her thumbs.

"Loving, intelligent, beautiful, funny, the usual stuff."

April nodded. Her eyes were very green. They hadn't

always been. I realized she was wearing tinted contacts. She said, "Boy, are you in love, huh?"

I nodded. April's eyes moved over the room again and stopped. She was looking at the back of a tall black man sitting at the counter eating a croissant. Her eyes moved on. The waiter brought her eggs and my sandwich.

"I love eggs Benedict," April said.

"How come you didn't order them?" I said. "I might have ordered you Raisin Bran or something."

She giggled. "Oh, you would not."

We ate a little. The tall black guy at the counter finished his croissant and had a second pot of tea. While he waited for it he looked aimlessly around the room, his eyes passing over us with no flicker of hesitation. He was slender. His hair was cut short and his thin mustache was carefully trimmed. His pale beige linen suit was stylishly loose. His shirt was an off-white, his tie was a shiny beige silk, and his shoes were light tan with pointed toes. His skin was the color of coffee with milk. Talk about color-coordinated.

"So you still haven't told me," April said, "what you're doing here in town."

"Patricia Utley called me, told me you'd left and she couldn't find you."

"She knows where I am," April said. "I talked with Steven."

"When he found you."

"I'm a big girl now," April said. "I don't have to tell everybody everything I'm doing."

"That's true," I said.

"So why are you here?"

"Well, at first I came down to find you, in case something bad had happened, but now I get here and you're okay, I just wanted to make sure you'd made a wise career move."

"I know what I'm doing," April said.

"That puts you one up on me," I said. "How come you decided to make the change?"

She poked at her eggs with the points of her fork. She made a small shrugging motion, like a bad habit almost broken.

"How'd you hear about Tiger Lilies?" I said.

"A guy I know," April said.

"And the minute you heard the name you were enthralled," I said.

She poked at her eggs some more, her shoulders frozen in their semi-shrug.

"I've got to be a part of it, you said. Tiger Lilies are my life, you said."

April shook her head. "No," she said. "You don't have to make fun of me. It wasn't like that."

"So what was it?"

"Like I told you, it was a guy I knew."

"He wanted you to work for Tiger Lilies?"

"He said it would be good for me," April said.

"Was he right?"

April nodded vigorously.

"Will it be good for you next year?"

April frowned. "Of course," she said.

"How can you be sure?"

"He says so."

"How do you know he's right?"

"He loves me," April said. She looked straight at me. "And I love him."

"What could be better," I said.

"You're in love," she said.

I nodded.

"Well, I am too. You think a hooker can't be in love?"

"With a guy who wants you to keep hooking?" I said.

"He's a musician. He's studying at Juilliard. As soon as he starts making money, I'll quit. Right now it's something I can do for him."

"Juilliard?" I said.

"Yes. You don't know what Juilliard is? It's just the best music school in the world."

"I know what Juilliard is," I said.

"And what I do when I'm hooking is just my job. It's not anything like what we do."

"You and the musician?"

She nodded hard. "That's right. What we do is love."

"What's the musician's name?"

"Why do you want to know?"

"I hate calling him the musician," I said. "What if I have to give the bride away?"

She paused. Her eyes flickered toward the counter. A woman wearing a lavender cape and a huge hat came in, paused on the platform, then swept down into the restaurant. It was like watching *The Loretta Young Show.*

"His name's Robert," she said.

"Not Bob?"

"No, he hates Bob. His name is Robert. Robert Rambeaux."

I finished off the first half of my sandwich. April had eaten one egg. The monochromatic man had another pot of tea at the counter. If he wasn't Robert Rambeaux, then I wasn't puckish and adorable.

"I'll try once," I said, "and then I'll get off your ass. What I know about the, ah, human condition tells me that a man doesn't love a woman if he turns her out to hook."

April's face started to close down.

"What I hear from Patricia Utley is that this place, Tiger Lilies, will use you up and sell you down scale. And old musical Robert Rambeaux will go out and recruit somebody else."

Tears had formed in April's eyes. "You fucking prick," she said. She stood up and turned away and walked up the stairs and out the door without even pausing for a pose.

So much for puckish and adorable.

I paid the check and finished my coffee and went out. Going out it's easier not to pose. I was halfway to the corner of 53rd and Park when the monochromatic man came out through the revolving door and walked along behind me. I walked up Park toward 59th Street. He cruised along behind me, sampling the spring air, admiring the young women in their spring clothes, checking out the elegance of the avenue. If he were any more casual, he'd have fallen down. He was about as subtle as Jesse Helms.

I turned west on 59th Street and walked two blocks to 59th and Fifth. The Plaza. Central Park. The Pierre just up the street. The Trump Tower just down the street. The great big city's a wondrous toy. Mr. Monochrome studied the artifacts in the window of A la Vieille Russie behind me. The light changed and I crossed and went into the park. Monochrome followed me.

There were people roller-skating in the park, and people with enormous tape players on their shoulders, and people with all their gear stuffed in a shopping bag. There were pretzel vendors and people walking Irish wolfhounds, and some joggers, and two guys sharing a pint of something from a paper bag on a bench. I went past them and found an empty bench and sat down. Monochrome walked past me and looked around and turned and walked back toward me. I gestured toward the empty space beside me. He ignored it and stood looking down at me. I smiled at him.

"Beige," I said.

He said, "How come you're bothering my lady?"

"Ah, it is you, Robert Rambeaux."

"What do you want, bothering her?"

"I was hoping she could get me tickets to your next recital," I said.

Rambeaux sighed and shook his head. "Everybody's a wiseass," he said.

"Now don't generalize, Bob," I said. "All that has been established here is that I am a wiseass."

"Robert," he said. The correction was automatic. "I asked you a question, whitebread, and I want an answer."

"White bread, Bobby? Racial taunts? You're about as black as Grace Kelly."

"I ought to kick your ass for you right here."

"Little question of that, Bobb-o," I said. "But you can't. And if you try, you're just going to get your outfit all wrinkled and sweaty."

Robert stepped about a step away and looked at me thoughtfully.

"You're a cocky motherfucker, aren't you," he said.

I shrugged. "It's just hard for me to get serious about a guy whose outfit took three hours to assemble."

"I'm tired of bullshitting around," Robert said. "I don't want you comin' near April again. You understand?"

"You really go to Juilliard?" I said.

"You understand?"

"I bet you don't," I said. "I bet you're a pimp instead."

Robert went inside the coat of his beige outfit and came out with a straight razor. He held it like he knew how.

"You better listen what I'm telling you, whitey."

"Heavenly days," I said, "talk about ethnic stereotyping."

"You go on back to Boston, fishbelly, and stay there and don't you come near my lady again."

I was still sitting. I put my left foot behind his right ankle, put my right foot against his right knee, pulled with the left, pushed with the right, and Robert went over backward. I stood up and stomped the razor out of his hand. I got a little of the hand in the process and Robert yelped.

"There goes your violin career," I said.

He came up swinging and he was better than he looked, with a lot of fluid speed in his punches. He was almost fast enough to hit me. I caught a punch on my right shoulder and rolled my chin away from another one and hit him in the solar plexus and he doubled over and backed away, holding his stomach, gasping.

"See why I'm cocky," I said.

His eyes scanned for the razor. It was ten feet away on the ground. It might as well have been in Paramus. Still bent over, he looked at me as the semiparalysis began to ease.

"What the fuck you want, man?" he said.

"Mostly I want to know that April Kyle is all right, and is going to stay all right."

Robert had straightened up. His shoulders were still a little forward and he was massaging his stomach with his right hand. But he could breathe.

"She's a fucking chippy, man. How all right do chippies get? How long they stay all right, you know?"

Two black kids on skateboards zipped between us and on down the walk.

"I didn't turn her out, man. She was a chippy 'fore I knew her."

I nodded. "Everything's relative," I said. "I don't want her worse off than she was."

"Hey, she's better off. She's making better bread than she ever made with Utley."

"And keeping it?" I said.

"Sure, man, whatta you think, I'm no pimp."

"Yeah, sure," I said, "you're a music student. You probably carry that razor to trim clarinet reeds."

"No shit, man. I'm taking courses at Juilliard."

"Robert," I said, "what's the point? If I can talk her out of you, I will. If you can stop me, you will."

"You can't talk her out of me, man."

"Probably not," I said. "But I'll try. And if you try to cut me again, I'll break both your arms."

"Maybe next time I won't be alone, man."

I turned back toward Fifth Avenue. "I think we can count on that, Rob," I said.

4

I strolled across the park toward Lincoln Center. To my left the row of high-rise hotels on 59th Street gleamed in benign elegance over the burgeoning green swales of Olmsted's grand design. Roller skaters and Walkmen and joggers and Frisbees and dogs and kerchiefs. Lunch in brown bags and park rangers on horseback and outcroppings of dark rock on which people sat and got the early yellow splash of spring sun in their faces. Birds sang. Maybe ten years ago a group of young men raped a young woman in the park and left her naked, gagged, and bound hand and foot. Another group of young men came along and found her and raped her too.

Ah wilderness.

Lincoln Center looked like an expensive complex of Turkish bathhouses, a compendium of neo-Arabic–Spanish and silly. It did for the West Side what the Trump Tower did for the East, offering the chance for a giggle on even the drabbest day.

A large-eyed woman wearing a full skirt and silver New Balance running shoes opened a file folder and told me that in fact Robert Rambeaux was registered at Juilliard. He was taking a course in composition with a practicum in woodwinds.

"What's his address?" I said. "He still living on First Street?"

"I'm sorry, sir, it's against our policy to give out that sort of information."

"Quite right," I said. "People drive you crazy if they know where you live. A person has a right to privacy."

She smiled at me and nodded. Her hair was pulled back behind her ears and fell to her shoulders. She didn't look very old, but there were gray streaks in her hair. Premature. Probably from worrying about the rights of privacy.

She had a cup of coffee in a white mug with Beethoven's picture on it. As I stood I brushed it with my elbow and spilled it across her desk and onto her lap.

She jumped up, trying to keep the coffee from soaking through, brushing her skirt with both hands.

"Oh, my God," I said. "I am sorry." While I said that I shuffled the stuff on top of her desk frantically out of the way, and in doing so I copped the top sheet out of Rambeaux's folder and folded it inside my jacket.

"It's all right," she said, her graying head still bent over, smoothing at her skirt. "Really, it's all right. The skirt is washable."

I closed Rambeaux's folder and put it and two other folders and a long pad of yellow paper in a pile on the corner of the desk. She left her skirt and turned her attention to the calculator on her desk, wiping it off with Kleenex she took from a drawer.

"Really," she said, "it's my fault. I shouldn't have left the coffee there. It'll be fine. I'll just get a wet paper towel from the ladies' room and wipe off the desk."

"Well," I said, "thanks for being so decent about it."

"No, really," she said.

I smiled my earnest smile at her and thanked her again and she put her file folders away in the file and locked it and went to the ladies' room to get a paper towel. I left.

Walking through Columbus Circle, I read Rambeaux's transcript. He'd done well in his courses. And he lived on East 77th Street. I put the transcript in a trash bin attached to a lamppost. Incriminating evidence. Probably could have looked Rambeaux up in the phone book. How many Robert Rambeauxs could there be? But it's good to keep in practice. And the risk factor at Juilliard was low.

I walked back across the park and crossed Fifth Avenue and turned uptown. There was a plate glass window on the Hotel Pierre and I checked my reflection as I went by. I was wearing a leather jacket and a blue-toned Allen Solly tattersall shirt and jeans, and Nike running shoes with a charcoal swoosh. I paused and turned the collar up on my leather jacket. Perfect. Did the traffic slow on Fifth Avenue to look at me? Maybe.

It was nearly four in the afternoon and getting less springlike when I turned east on 77th Street. I crossed Madison Avenue, the Hotel Carlyle on the southeast corner. Rambeaux's building was five and a half blocks east. Between Second and First avenues, a five-story gray brick building with black iron fire escapes zigzagging the front. The bell directory listed Rambeaux in 5D. I settled into the entryway of a brownstone church across the street and waited.

Rambeaux knew me, so it would be harder following him. But not so hard it couldn't be done. I zipped my jacket up. It pulled a little tight over my shoulder holster, and it lost the nice contrast with my Allen Solly shirt. But the alternative was coldness. It's almost never perfect. After five, people began coming home. Students with school bags and musical instruments in cases, young women in tailored suits with blouses and bows at the neck, young men in tailored suits and white shirts and ties at the neck. A lot of briefcases. Nothing happened across the street. It was a quarter to six, it was chilly, I was missing the cocktail hour. Soon I would be missing the supper hour.

At six-twenty Rambeaux came out of the house wearing a tweed coat with a velvet collar. There was a young woman with him. It wasn't April. They walked to Second Avenue and caught a cab downtown. I drifted along behind them and caught the next one.

"I can't think of a slick way to put this," I said to the cabbie, "but follow that cab."

The driver turned toward me and said, "Where you go?"

"Follow that cab," I said.

"La Guardia?" he said. "Grann Central? Waldorf?"

"Allez-vous après ce taxi?" I said.

He shook his head. Rambeaux's cab took a right turn on 75th Street.

"Never mind," I said and got out of the cab and started across Second.

"Som a beetch," the cabbie yelled after me, out the passenger window.

"Sonova," I said. "Son . . . of . . . a . . . bitch. Short *i*."

The cabbie pulled away, spinning a little rubber as he went. I walked back to the St. Regis. *Follow that cab.* It seemed simple enough. Used to work perfect for Richard Arlen.

5

The next morning I went over to the Hertz place on West 56th Street and rented a tan Toyota Celica, and drove up to 77th Street and parked across the street from Rambeaux's place, in front of a hydrant, with the nose of the Toyota aimed at Second Avenue. I let the motor idle, and listened to WNEW and ate two bagels with cream cheese and drank coffee. I had on jeans again and my leather jacket and my Nikes, standard tracking outfit. But I had changed my shirt and was wearing my Utica Blue Sox baseball hat for disguise. Also because it made me look stunning. William B. Williams was just saying that WNEW was where it all began when Rambeaux emerged from his building. It was nearly noon. He turned toward First Avenue. God damn. I pulled the Toyota out from the hydrant, ran the light turning left onto Second Avenue, made the light turning left onto 76th Street, and ran the light turning onto First Avenue. Many New Yorkers honked at me. But ahead of me Rambeaux was just getting into a cab and heading uptown.

Follow that cab.

We went to 87th Street, where Rambeaux picked up a young black woman with her hair pulled tight in a chignon, who was waiting on the corner. Then we went crosstown to Fifth Avenue and back downtown to 76th Street. Rambeaux paid off the cab and he and the lady walked down 76th Street. I edged around the corner and double-parked behind a truck that said it delivered Boars Head sausage. Rambeaux and the young lady went into a restaurant near the corner of 76th and Madison, Les Pleiades. It didn't look like a place where jeans and a Utica Blue Sox cap would pass unnoticed, so I waited behind the Boars Head sausage truck for an hour and forty-five minutes.

I'd once eaten lunch in Les Pleiades. I had had a lamb stew with *haricots verts* and several bottles of Fisher beer. Maybe they were having that, or fresh asparagus with the butts carefully peeled, served with a mild vinaigrette. At ten of two they came out and caught a cab and went back to her place on 87th Street. Rambeaux went in. He came out at four and walked back to his apartment with me dawdling several blocks back, annoying hell out of maybe thirty-five cab drivers. At four-twenty he turned into his building and I was back at my spot on the hydrant. At four thirty-five an NYPD patrol car pulled up with two cops in it and the one on the passenger side told me to move away from the hydrant. I nodded and smiled and apologized and pulled out behind them and went around the block and parked on the hydrant again.

By a quarter of seven I was giving some thought to eating my Utica Blue Sox hat, and maybe would have but for the stunningness issue. Two bagels don't cover you into the evening. At ten of seven Rambeaux came out. He had on a vanilla-colored double-breasted suit and a dark shirt open at the throat and carried a black trench coat over his arm. He went up toward Second Avenue. If he caught a cab there, I'd follow in the car. He didn't, he went on across Second. I left the Toyota on the hydrant and followed him on foot. He was walking. If he were going uptown, he'd have caught a cab on First. If he were heading crosstown, he'd have hailed one on the corner. At Lexington he went into the subway and I followed him. He put a token into the slot and I did too. I always got a few tokens when I was tailing someone. Be prepared. I got on a car behind the one Rambeaux got on, and watched him sort of obliquely through the connecting doors. The subway wasn't jammed, but there were enough people so blending in was easy. We got out at 42nd Street and walked west. I stayed on the other side of the street and kept my head down, but Rambeaux wasn't nervous. There was a spring in his step and he made no attempt to evade a tail. He had no reason to think there'd be one. He never looked around. When we crossed Fifth Avenue past the library and began to move toward Times Square the spring in Rambeaux's step seemed to increase. At Sixth Avenue he seemed barely to touch the ground, and by the time we got to Times Square he was clearly in a New York state of mind. Times Square is the Parthenon of sleaze. And Rambeaux seemed right in his element. He moved easily among the porn theaters and shops that sell ghetto blasters and martial arts equipment. He paused, spoke to a black woman in a red leather miniskirt and a blond wig, moved on, talked to a young girl in a black leather miniskirt and white mesh stockings, moved on and stood in the doorway of a store that sold adult novelty items, his arms folded, a look of benign pleasure on his face. He bobbed his head slightly, probably listening to the lullaby of Broadway. A chunky white man in a three-piece suit stopped to speak to him. Rambeaux smiled and shook his head. The man walked on. Rambeaux's eyes ranged across the square and then he arched his back in a stretching movement, and moved out and walked uptown along Broadway. He paused, traded a low five with a burly black man in a safari jacket, talked for a moment, took a cigarette and moved along toward 44th Street smoking. At the corner of 44th Street he spoke with two women, both in miniskirts and boots, one of them wearing a squirrel jacket, the other coatless, wearing a scoop-neck sequined blouse. One woman was white, the other oriental. He took the hand of the oriental girl and held it for a minute. I saw her face tighten in pain and realized he was squeezing it. Then he dropped her hand and smiled and kissed each of them on the cheek and drifted on up Broadway. Rambeaux was the home office. He was making a field inspection.

At 50th Street, Rambeaux crossed and worked that side of Broadway back toward 42nd. He smoked several cigarettes. He talked with whores, occasionally spoke with a colleague. As the evening cooled he slipped on his black trench coat, cut fashionably large, with a belt around the waist. There were fast-food joints and I was in danger of malnutritive hallucinations, but anything cooked in Times Square would probably give you rabies.

By ten I knew what I needed to know. Rambeaux was a pimp and he had a string of streetwalkers. Who the young ladies were he'd dined with uptown was not yet clear. But I knew what was happening here. I revisited two or three of the girls on my own and made sure I'd recognize them. Then I walked over to Sixth Avenue and caught a cab up to 77th Street and retrieved my car. The Hertz Corp. had gotten a ticket. Serves them right, parking on a hydrant. I put the ticket in the glove compartment and returned the car and went to the St. Regis with visions of the room service menu dancing in my head.

6

Times Square at eight-fifteen in the morning is as sleazy as it is at night. And as busy. The whores were out getting an early start on the daily quota. Several winos had managed to get drunk already. Everywhere the industrious among us were up and at it. Me too. I was talking with the youngish whore in the black miniskirt and white mesh stockings I'd seen talking last night to Rambeaux.

"What are you interested in?" she said.

"Baseball, English landscape paintings, beer. How 'bout yourself?"

She shook her head. She was tired and even my lyrical wit didn't seem to brighten her face.

"You want action or not?" she said.

"I want to buy you breakfast and talk with you," I said.

She shrugged. "It's an hourly rate," she said. "What you do with your time is up to you."

"Okay," I said, and paid her. "Now you're mine until nine twenty-five."

"Sure thing, sugar. Where we going?"

"How about the HoJo," I said. "Across the square."

"Sure."

We crossed Broadway and Seventh where they intersect and walked up to the Howard Johnson's and sat in a booth. I had black coffee. She had scrambled eggs and sausage patties, two strips of bacon, and home fries, buttered toast, and a Coke.

"Take care of any cholesterol deficiency you might be suffering," I said.

"Sure," she said. "What you want to talk about?"

"What's your name?" I said.

"Ginger." She used a toast triangle to push some scrambled eggs onto her fork.

"How long you been hooking, Ginger?"

She shrugged while she swallowed her eggs. "Long time," she said.

"Always with Rambeaux?"

She stopped eating and stared at me. "You know him?"

"Sure," I said.

"You and him ain't friends," she said.

"True, but I know him."

"You a cop?"

"No."

"The hell you ain't," Ginger said.

"I'm not a cop. I'm not going to arrest anybody. I'm looking for information."

"You're a fucking cop," Ginger said. "You think I don't know a cop."

She ate some more of her scrambled eggs. It didn't bother her a hell of a lot if I was a cop. Cops were just another itch to scratch. If I busted her, the pimp would bail her out and she'd be back at work tomorrow. "You want to shake Robert down?" Ginger said.

"No. I want to find out a little about him."

"How come?" She finished her eggs and sausage, and was nibbling a limp bacon slice in her fingers.

"Girl I know is in love with him. I want to see if he's reliable."

Ginger put down her bacon slice and wiped her fingers on a napkin. She sat back in the booth and stared at me.

"Reliable?"

"Yeah," I said, "reliable."

She smiled briefly. "You can rely on Robert," she said. "You can rely on him to make every dime he can off your body and never let go of it until he can't make anything more. He's reliable as hell about that."

"That's sort of what I was afraid of."

"What do you think he's like. He's a pimp. You think pimps are reliable?"

"How'd you meet him?" I said.

Ginger ate the rest of her bacon. I waited while she did. I still had forty minutes left on the meter and I could always buy another hour. A waitress filled my coffee cup. Ginger sat back in the booth again and sipped her Coke.

"I was working in a house in Boston."

"And?"

The waitress came back and put the check down.

"I'm sick of sitting here," Ginger said. "Let's get out of here."

I paid the check and we were on the street again. The weather was pleasant. Warm enough for Ginger's skirt and sleeveless sequined top.

"Anywhere you want to go?" I said.

"Someplace else," she said.

"How about the zoo?" I said.

She glanced around Times Square. "How different can it be," she said.

I got us a cab and we rode in silence to Central Park. The cabbie dropped us at Columbus Circle and we walked across the park, east, toward the zoo. Ginger's costume looked less appropriate in the park, but no one seemed to notice. New York offers the gift of loneliness, E. B. White had said once.

We were standing in front of the polar bear cage when I said again, "And?"

Ginger seemed startled. "And what?" she said.

"And you met Rambeaux, what then?"

She looked at her watch. "You gonna pay me some more?"

"Yes," I said. "Just leave the meter running. I'll pay you for all the time it takes."

She nodded. She looked at the bear. "You think he likes it in there?"

"No," I said. "I think he'd rather be up on the polar ice cap hotfooting it after a seal. What happened after you met Sweet Robert?"

"I came to New York with him."

"Because?"

"Because I came."

"Better money?" I said.

She was watching the bear. "Something like that," she said.

"Was it that?"

She still watched the bear. I watched him too. He had a beer keg in the water with him and he mauled it and rolled over it, taking it under and letting it pop up. It wasn't much but what the hell else was there to do?

After a long time, Ginger said, "No."

"It wasn't money?"

"No."

"It was love," I said.

"I'm sick of looking at this fucking bear," she said.

"Sure."

We moved toward the monkey house. In front of a cage full of capuchin monkeys Ginger turned and leaned her fanny on the railing and said, "Yeah. It was love."

"Better reason than money," I said.

"Bullshit," Ginger said. "Men think shit like that. Women don't."

"Hard to generalize," I said. "What happened when you got to New York?"

"He put me on the street."

"Now, that's love," I said.

Ginger looked past me at the monkeys in the cage across the aisle. She didn't say anything.

"Sorry," I said.

She looked back at me silently and nodded.

"So you were on the street."

"Robert was studying music and he needed time and so I split my money with him."

"And what did he contribute?"

"I thought he loved me," Ginger said. "And he was protection."

"Against what?"

"Whatever. He'd hang around in case the john was freaky. Or tried to rip us off. Make sure I came out when I was supposed to. Stuff like that."

We walked toward the lions. On the other side of the pit was a guy selling popcorn. "You want some?" I said.

"Sure," Ginger said.

I left her leaning on the railing looking at the lions and walked over to the popcorn cart. When I came back two teenage Hispanic kids were talking to her. The heavier of them made a kissing sound with his lips and rubbed his thumb across his fingertips. He had on a yellow silk jacket. I handed Ginger the popcorn. And looked at the two kids.

"She wit' you, man?"

I nodded.

"We thought she was alone, man." Both kids were much shorter than I was and I was looking down at them. Always effective. I kept looking. The kid in the yellow jacket shrugged and he and his pal swaggered away.

"I'm impressed," Ginger said.

"At what?"

"You. You must be fairly scary. Kids like that aren't normally scared of anything."

"They are, they pretend they're not," I said.

"With you they didn't pretend. They must have seen something."

"They probably sensed I am pure of heart," I said. "What happened? How come you're not in a classy call house? Why'd he turn you out on the street?"

She shrugged again. In the strong sunlight there were small wrinkles around her eyes. Her makeup looked harsh.

"He says I'm shopworn," she said.

I raised my eyebrows.

She nodded and ate some popcorn. She held the box out toward me. I shook my head.

"So Rambeaux moved you down scale."

"Un huh. A lot less money per trick."

"So more tricks," I said.

"Robert's tuition payments didn't drop," she said.

"They never will," I said.

"Tell me something I don't know," Ginger said.

"And when you get a little more shopworn?"

"There's a place in Miami," she said, "where the girls never get out of bed. Guys get fifteen minutes, by the clock, then a bell rings and they gotta get off, and the next guy gets on."

"A little short on foreplay," I said.

"It's a living," Ginger said.

"No," I said. "It isn't."

7

We were in a place on Seventh Avenue called Freddy's, sitting at the bar. Ginger was drinking a Tequila Sunrise.

"Robert doesn't check me during the day," Ginger said. "He has an idea how much I should average, I don't come up with it and he gets sort of nasty."

I had a draft beer. I took a small sip. It was only two in the afternoon. I had a long day ahead.

"So he don't care. I'll give him a nice take for today. He don't care if I earn it fucking or talking."

"Except about him," I said.

Ginger's eyes got rounder and she stared at me. "He won't know that," she said.

"Not from me," I said.

She drank some more of her drink, and looked at the bartender. He nodded and brought her another one.

"He can be awful mean," Ginger said.

"Musicians are sensitive," I said. "They're easily upset."

"Shit," Ginger said. There was a big purple bruise on her upper right arm. But she had that kind of pale northern European skin that bruises easily and she may have earned the bruise in plying her trade.

"You like this work, Ginger?"

She laughed silently. "You from Social Services?"

"So it's a corny question. I still want to know. You like the work?"

Ginger examined the surface tension on her Tequila Sunrise. She took a deep breath, and let it out. "I used to," she said. "I'd turn maybe ten tricks a day. Okay guys. Clean. Wives out in the suburbs. No trouble."

"Good money?"

"Yeah, great. Fifty to a hundred thousand a year. A lot of the tricks were party stuff. Guy wanted to get it on with two of us. Guy wanted to do some coke, drink some booze." She motioned to the bartender for another Sunrise. "Sometimes they'd get so blown away they couldn't even get it up." The bartender brought the drink. I stayed with my beer, a sip at a time. "Lot of them couldn't get it up even sober. Want to watch a couple of girls french each other. So okay, fine with me. Dough's the same whatever I'm eating, you know?" Ginger finished her drink and picked up the new one. The bar was quiet in the midafternoon, dark and cool and full of the dull gleam of bottles and mahogany and brass and Naugahyde.

"You got a cigarette?" Ginger said.

"No, but I can buy some."

"Yeah. Marlboros in a box."

The bartender gave us the cigarettes. Ginger took one out. The bartender lit it for her and left the matches. Ginger took a long drag. "I only smoke when I'm drinking," she said.

"It might be nice with something cool," I said.

She nodded, looking past me toward the window where the light from Seventh Avenue filtered through the tinted glass.

"A lot of them like to be chained," she said. "They'd crawl around and bark like a dog and get off in their pants." Ginger snorted a humorless kind of snort. "Assholes," she said. "They'd want you to spank them." She shook her head, listening to herself talk. Not paying me much attention. "Not many good bodies. Mostly fat, white, lot of them had hairy backs." She looked at me. "You probably got a good body," she said.

"Schwarzenegger," I said. "Think Arnold Schwarzenegger."

"You scared hell out of those two spick kids," she said.

"You still like the work?" I said.

"It's work," she said. "What the hell else can I do?"

"Tend bar," I said.

"Big deal. Slopping drinks to a bunch of fucking lushes. At least I got someone looking out for me. Who looks out for you when you tend bar?"

I shook my head. "Robert's looking out for you?"

She laughed again. "He's looking out for him."

"So how much is he looking out for you?"

"He needs me. He takes care of business."

"If you tended bar," I said, "I suppose you'd have to look out for yourself. You and the union."

"That shit's okay if you're a man," Ginger said.

I nodded. A middle-aged man came into the bar wearing brand-new cowboy boots, and Sergio Valente jeans, with his hair blow-dried and his shirt collar carefully smoothed out over the lapels of his suede sport coat. His wife's jeans were tucked into her boots. The jeans were too tight and plainly revealed the spandex undergarment that compressed her butt. The mass of black hair piled on her head seemed to dwarf her face. Visitors in the big city. Up from Orlando, maybe. Or in from Wilkes-Barre, or Worcester.

"What did you do before you started hooking?" I said.

"Nothing." Ginger made a kind of shivery motion. "How come you want to know all this shit?"

"I don't know much about whores and this kid I'm interested in is one. I thought I'd better inform myself."

"Why don't you ask her?"

"She doesn't know what you know," I said.

"She will."

"Maybe not," I said.

"You gonna save her?"

"Maybe," I said.

Ginger laughed her joyless laugh.

"Why?" she said.

"Why not?"

"You gonna save me?"

"Maybe," I said.

Ginger was still for a moment. Then she said, "Shit," and drank her Tequila Sunrise.

8

From the window of my room at the St. Regis I could see Fifth Avenue. It was early evening and the crowd on the street was on its way to early dinner, or late shopping. The sky beyond the skyscrapers to the west was still light, but down in the city it was dark and the streetlights were on.

I turned from the window and looked at Ginger. She was sitting on the edge of the bed eating a cheeseburger and drinking beer. The room service table was in front of her with a pink tablecloth and a rose in a glass vase.

"What about Robert?" I said.

"Fuck him," Ginger said. "He don't own me. I give him his cut, what difference does it make to him?"

"Doesn't he like to know where you are?"

She chewed a bite of her sandwich and swallowed and pulled at the beer bottle.

"Who gives a shit what he likes. He'll get his share."

"Is he going to be nasty about this?" I said.

She tossed her head a little. "I can handle him."

I nodded and picked up a half a turkey and Swiss

cheese sandwich on pumpernickel. I took a bite, leaning my hips against the windowsill. Ginger ate a french fry with her fingers. She drank some more beer.

"How'd you get into this line of work?" I said.

"Jesus, you don't quit," Ginger said, "do you."

I shook my head.

"You really worried about this new hooker, huh?"

I nodded.

She ate another french fry. "There more beer?" she said.

"Sure," I said, and got one from the ice bucket and opened it and handed it to her. She drank it from the bottle.

"What the hell is she to you?" Ginger said. "She been hauling your ashes for you? You jealous of Robert?"

I shook my head.

"You married?" Ginger said.

"No."

"Girlfriend?"

"Yes."

"But she's kinda cold, right? Don't like the kinky stuff. So you have to hustle a little on the side, buy a little strange pussy now and then and tell yourself you're saving her."

"How'd you get into the business?" I said.

Ginger drank from the bottle. She picked a piece of

congealed melted cheese from the plate and ate it and drank some more beer.

"Fuck you," she said. "You want to save some floozie, go ahead, save her yourself. I don't have to tell you shit."

"How come you can't tell me how you got into hooking?"

" 'Cause it's none of your fucking business," Ginger said. "You probably one of those creeps likes to get off hearing about it. I thought you was gonna save me."

"Not if you're where you want to be."

"Goddamned right," Ginger said. "I'm where I want to be. I could show you some goddamned tricks too. You think I'm not good?"

"Good's not what you do," I said. "It's how you feel when you do it."

"You think so, huh."

I nodded. Ginger ate the rest of her cheeseburger. I was quiet. When she finished she wiped her mouth with a napkin. Then she drank some beer and wiped her mouth again, and looked at me across the table.

"Let me tell you something, you smug son of a bitch," she said. Eating and drinking and wiping her mouth had smeared away most of her lipstick. Behind me, down in the street, a bus downshifted. A horn sounded. Ginger closed her mouth and opened it and nothing came out. As I watched her, tears began to fill her eyes and when they had filled her eyes they began to run down her cheeks. She seemed to be trying to get her breath in big sighs, then she put her face in her hands and bent forward and rested her forehead on the room service table in the space between her cheeseburger plate and the water glass, and sobbed. The sobbing became harsher and her shoulders shook. A fork fell off the table and onto the floor and a water glass tipped and wet her hair and she didn't stop sobbing.

I went over and moved the table away and sat on the bed beside her and put my arm around her. She pressed her face against my chest and sobbed. I patted her hair.

She cried for maybe ten minutes, her chest heaving, gasping for air, her left hand clutched onto my shirt front, her right holding on to my back. Then she stopped sobbing and her body began to shake less. Then it stopped. Then her breathing began to get more controlled. Deep breaths but regular.

With her face still pressed against my chest she said, "My father's name is Vern Buckey, toughest man in Lindell, Maine. When I was a little kid he used to fool around with me, by the time I was twelve he was dicking me." I patted her hair.

"My old lady knew about it but she was scared to say anything. Everybody knew about it. Kids used to call me Fucky Buckey. But nobody did anything about it. Everybody was scared of Vern. When I was fourteen he sold me to a whorehouse in Portland."

The overhead light was on. It had seemed cheerful in the gathering evening, with the room service table being wheeled in. Now it seemed too bright. Like the lights in an operating room. But I couldn't reach the switch, so I sat still in the harsh light and patted Ginger's hair and let her clutch me and didn't say anything at all.

9

Ginger and I slept apart on the same bed. In the morning I gave her most of my cash and put her in a cab. She gave me her phone number. I gave her my card.

"You need me, you call me," I said.

She nodded. Since she'd told me about her father she hadn't said five words. The cab pulled away and I watched it turn downtown on Fifth Avenue. *Vern Buckey, Lindell, Maine.* I got in the next cab and went to Patricia Utley's town house on 37th Street, west of Lexington. It was as elegant and quiet as it had been ten years ago when I'd come here looking for another young woman.

Steven let me in. Patricia Utley was waiting in her library. There was a silver service for two laid out with coffee and some half-size croissants.

"Have you breakfasted?" she said.

"No, ma'am, but, begging your pardon, this don't look like it."

She smiled. "Shall I have Steven bring some Froot Loops?" She poured coffee from the silver pot into a white china cup with a silver band around the rim. I ate a croissant.

"Do I have to save any for you?" I said.

"Perhaps one," Patricia said. "Have you spoken with April?"

"Yeah. She's in love with a pimp named Robert Rambeaux, who studies music at Juilliard and needs her money to complete his education."

Patricia poured herself some coffee.

"I met Rambeaux," I said. "Tall, lean, light-colored man of African ancestry. Thinks he's tough, carries a straight razor. He told me to stop bothering his lady."

"Did you agree?"

"No. Robert and I agreed to disagree."

She smiled and took a small lump of sugar from a small silver bowl with small silver tongs and dropped it into her coffee.

"And?" she said.

"And I tailed him and noticed that he spends a lot of time with attractive young women during the day and that he runs a string of streetwalkers at night."

Patricia said, "He turns the girls over to a high-class service and takes the used ones and turns them out for himself. He gets a commission from the high-class house and he gets the income from the street girls. It's quite a profitable arrangement."

"Like a car dealer," I said. "Sells you a new car, takes your car in trade and sells it. Gets a double profit."

Patricia nodded.

"The funny thing is," I said, "he really is enrolled at Juilliard."

"People aren't one thing," Patricia said.

"Yeah, I know. Hitler loved dogs."

"He probably did in fact," Patricia Utley said.

"Didn't make him not Hitler," I said.

"True."

"I met one of the street whores. Kid named Ginger Buckey. Actually not so much a kid anymore. Except by my standards."

"Our standards," Patricia Utley said. "We're about the same age."

"But we don't look it. She asked me if I was going to save her."

"And you think you can?" Patricia Utley said.

"No," I said. "That's what makes it lousy. I know I can't."

Patricia took a very small bite off the narrow end of one of the croissants. "Care to tell me about her?" she said.

I did.

When I was through Patricia Utley said, "And you have noted her father's name?"

"Vern Buckey," I said.

"And where he lives."

"Lindell, Maine," I said.

She smiled. "And you won't forget it."

"No."

She smiled more. "You are a piece of work," she said.

"Un huh."

"Oh, I know you won't race up to Maine burning with a passion to right old wrongs. You are in your own idealistic way as cynical as I am. But you'll store that up and maybe, someday, if you have occasion to go to Maine . . ."

I shrugged. "One never knows," I said.

"Perhaps the most charming part of it all is that it's not just because he was bestial to his child. It's that. But it's also because you would want to find out if he really is the toughest man in Lindell, Maine."

"For a person I see every ten years you seem to know a lot about me," I said.

"I know a great deal about men," she said.

"And I'm typical?"

"No, you are entirely untypical. You're not like other men and it makes you interesting and I think about you."

"Jeepers," I said.

"Filing away Vern Buckey's name for future reference is perfect you. You feel compassion for her suffering and anger at his cruelty and competition in his toughness. You want to save her, punish him, and prove you're tougher. Man/boy. Lover/killer. Savior/bully."

"When I run into Vern Buckey," I said, "I'm going to bust his ass for him."

Patricia Utley put her head back and laughed with pleasure. "I'm sure you will," she said. "And what I like best of all is after you've done it, you'll feel kind of bad for him."

"So what shall we do about April Kyle?" I said.

"Let her go," Patricia Utley said. "She loves this guy. She's having a good time. She's making a lot of money."

"Ginger said fifty to a hundred thousand," I said.

"Certainly," Patricia said. "If the girl is attractive and willing, she can make excellent pay. Even more if she is black or oriental."

"Black and oriental?"

"Yes. They are perceived as exotic and are in greater demand."

"Exotic," I said.

"There are not many jobs at which a woman, or a man for that matter, can make a hundred thousand a year," she said.

"For a while," I said.

"Certainly for a while. That's true of baseball players and ballet dancers as well."

"And then what. Ginger says there's a place in Miami where the girls never get out of bed."

"A slaughterhouse," Patricia Utley said. "Certainly.

There are such places. There's one in Paris, too. But such places are not necessarily the elephant graveyards of old whores. Some go into management." She smiled slightly and glanced at her library with its bookshelves crowded and the spring sun sprawling across her Afghan carpet. "Some marry and lead ordinary lives. You remember Donna Burlington."

"Aka Linda Rabb," I said. "Sure. It's how we met."

"Not all whores are full-time. There are many part-timers. Housewives who turn tricks in the afternoon while the kids are in school and the hubby is at work. Sometimes the husband knows. Sometimes he doesn't. There are college girls and actresses and models and computer programmers. I've employed all of the above and some others."

"Why do they do it?"

"Besides the money?"

"Yes."

"The money matters," Patricia Utley said. "I know it doesn't matter very much to you. But you have enough, and you're so self-sufficient that most things don't matter very much. But money matters a great deal to a lot of people, including me. It is power. It is freedom. It is a support and a security and a sense that you have tangible worth."

"I understand that, but what else?"

"Most whores don't like men very much," she said. "They are quite scornful of them."

"And the men?"

"I would say that most men who patronize whores don't like women very much."

"Intimate distaste," I said.

"Sex and power are pretty tightly connected," she said. "In ways I'm not sure even I understand. And I've had a close-up view for quite some years now."

"It doesn't explain why April loves Robert," I said.

"Or thinks she does," Patricia said.

"Maybe he could love her," I said.

Patricia Utley simply stared at me.

"Love comes in odd shapes sometimes," I said.

"Spenser," she said, "I don't know very much about love. But I know a hell of a lot about whores and pimps. April Kyle is in the machine. The machine will process her. When the process is through it won't have mattered whether she and Robert Rambeaux love each other or not. You are a man, and you are a romantic—which is probably two ways of saying the same thing. You think love is something. A thing. A force in human affairs. It is not a force in whore–pimp affairs. It's just another word for fucking."

"So why does April think she's in love?" I said.

"I don't know. I don't even care. I'm sick of the word. Isn't your girlfriend a shrink? Ask her."

The croissants were gone. So was the coffee. I sat quietly for a while.

"I can tell April what I know about Rambeaux," I said. "But . . ."

"She knows it already," Patricia said.

"Yes."

"It's all you can do," she said.

"Yeah."

She stood and put out her hand. "It was good to see you again."

I took her hand. "You too," I said.

We walked to the door. She opened it.

"I'll pay you for your time," she said.

"Better than paying me for results," I said.

10

April wasn't around. I tried Tiger Lilies Escort Service and they said she was not there. I asked where she was and they said they were sorry but they were not able to give me that information. I said I wanted to speak with the manager and they hung up. I looked her up in the Manhattan directory. There were twenty-seven Kyles but none named April. Perhaps Robert could help me locate her.

I cabbed up to 77th Street and rang his bell at three-thirty. It was after lunchtime and he was probably still in bed. I rang again and heard a voice badly muffled on the intercom. I said, "It's me," into the speaker. In a moment the door buzzed open. I knew he didn't know who "It's me" was any more than I'd recognize his voice. The sound was so distorted that you might be able to distinguish species and gender but no more than that.

I took the elevator to the fifth floor and looked at myself in the mirrored wall of the elevator till we got there. The hall was short. There were maybe four apartments to the floor. Opposite the elevator door was a stairwell, rimmed with a dark oaken railing. Rambeaux's apartment was to the left, in the front of the building. I knocked. I could hear a small rustle behind the door. And the peephole darkened. Then silence. I knocked again. No answer. I knocked again. The door opened a crack, held narrow by a chain.

"What the fuck you want?" Rambeaux said.

I could see just the strip of him that showed through the narrow door. "Ah, you syrup-tongued dandy," I said. "No wonder you're hell with the ladies."

"Whyn't you get fucking lost, huh?"

"I'm looking for April. She's not at Tiger Lilies and they won't say where she is."

"She's not here. I don't know where she is. Maybe out with a john."

"No," I said, "the way they said it was that she wasn't there. Like she wouldn't be there later, either."

"Maybe she don't want to see you."

"How cruel," I said, "but even if it were true, they didn't know who I was. I could have been a customer." I had leaned my shoulder against the door as I talked. I was wearing the gray Nikes with a charcoal swoosh, and putting my foot in the door didn't seem like the best way to deal with it. It was Nikes' only flaw.

Rambeaux pushed back. "I don't know where she is

and I don't want to," he said. "I got nothing to do with her anymore."

"What about tuition?" I said.

"Just get the fuck away from me, man." Rambeaux was pushing harder. "I got a gun."

He shifted behind the door and I saw the other side of his face through the opening. His left eye was closed and his cheek was swollen and discolored.

"Somebody beat you up?" I said.

"Nobody done shit," he said. "Please, man. Get the fuck away from me."

I relaxed my lean on the door for a minute and he closed the opening again. Then I pressed my right foot flat against the wall behind me and lunged the door inward. The chain pulled out of the doorjamb, screws and all, and the door flew open. Rambeaux bounced back against the wall, on the other side of the door, and I was in. I pulled the door away from him and closed it. Rambeaux did in fact have a gun. A squat blue short barreled S&W .32 that he held in front of him with both hands like they do on the cop shows.

I said, "Robert, if you need to steady that thing two-handed to hit me from eleven inches away you better think about a strength program."

"I'll use it, you bastard."

"I'm sure you would if you needed to," I said. "But you won't need to."

I turned and walked into his apartment. It was one room with a stand-up kitchen and a bathroom. Most of the bed-sitting-room was occupied by an unfolded sofa bed unmade with dark maroon silk sheets and a pale gray puff comforter.

Rambeaux still stood against the wall by the door with the short gun held in front of him. He was in his underwear, stretch bikinis with gray and maroon stripes. He was wiry and looked in shape but he was no bigger than a tall middleweight. In addition to the black eye, his lower lip was swollen. There was a purple blotch on his rib cage on the right side and a reddish welt on his forehead above his right eye.

"What's going on?" I said.

Rambeaux shook his head.

"I look for April, she's not around. I come here, you say you don't know where she is and you got nothing more to do with her. Day before yesterday you told me to stay away from your 'lady'—always one of my favorite expressions. Now you don't know where she is, don't want to know where she is, and you look like you were in a hatchet fight and didn't have a hatchet. There are inferences to be drawn."

Rambeaux let the gun drop to his side, holding it in

his right hand. He walked into the room and sat on the bed and looked at me, the gun resting on his thigh. He shook his head, and it must have hurt, because he stopped in midshake and began to massage the back of his neck with his free hand.

"Listen, man. Two days ago I was doing fine. I had a nice little connection for myself. Had some ladies working for me. Then you show up and everything is fucked up. You keep hanging around and we both gonna get killed and I done shit to deserve it."

"I try to use this power wisely," I said. "Who's going to kill us?"

Rambeaux shook his head. "I won't tell you nothing," he said. "I don't know where April is. I ain't going to know tomorrow neither. You can keep coming around and fucking with me but I still ain't going to know."

"But if you're seen with me it'll cause trouble?"

Rambeaux looked straight at me. His eyes were dark and shiny. "Stay away from me, man. Honest to God, I don't know nothing about April and you just going to get me killed for nothing."

He had the gun pointed at me again.

"Maybe not for nothing," I said.

"Jesus, man, she's just quiff, you know. I go out and in an hour I collect ten more just as good."

"So how come somebody punched your lights out

over her and how come you're scared of dying over her, and how come I can't find her?"

"Ain't her, man, it's who . . ." He shook his head. "No, you get out of here or I swear to God I'll shoot. I will waste you right fucking here."

I stood with my hands in my hip pockets and my back to the windows, with the light from the windows brightening the rumpled silk sheets, on the unfolded bed. Rambeaux had the gun up now in both hands again, pointed at the middle of my stomach. He was shivering.

"Okay," I said. "I'm going to leave you my card, in case you need to talk with me."

I took my wallet out and pulled a card free and left it on the maroon lacquered coffee table that had been pushed against the wall to make room for the bed.

"I don't want no card," Rambeaux said. "I don't want to see you again ever."

"In case," I said. "Maybe even in case you need help."

Rambeaux shook his head and stood, the gun pointed at me now held straight out in front with both hands.

"She alive?" I said.

Rambeaux nodded. "She fine, man, forget her."

I nodded toward my card on the coffee table. "In case you need help," I said, and walked out carefully past him.

I went down to Times Square then and looked for

Ginger Buckey but couldn't find her. I had dinner and went back and looked some more and still couldn't find her, so I went back to the hotel and went to bed. It was my most significant accomplishment of the day.

11

My motto is if at first you don't succeed, the hell with it. So, in the morning I packed and checked out and took the 10:00 A.M. shuttle back from New York. The shuttle runs between Boston and New York every hour on the hour and guarantees a seat. It is very convenient, usually late, and has size 42 seats, which can be difficult if you are a size 48 passenger. In Boston I got my car out of the parking garage and drove to my office.

I got a cup of coffee to go and took it upstairs with me and sat at my desk. There were several days' worth of letters piled under the mail slot. Most of them spelled my name wrong, none of them mattered and I threw the batch into my wastebasket.

I looked at my answering machine. The red message light glowed unblinking. No calls. I got up and opened both windows and looked out the window. I was still at the corner of Berkeley and Boylston streets, over a bank. Across the street the ad agency was still there, but Linda Thomas didn't work there anymore. They had a male art director now and I didn't know where Linda was. I drank some coffee. Spring air drifted into my office. Some exhaust fumes, too, but mostly spring air.

I sat down and made out a bill to Patricia Utley for my time and put it in an envelope and addressed it. I peeled a stamp out of the little plastic dispenser that holds one hundred that the post office will sell you for a nickel, except they almost never have them in stock. I put the stamp on the envelope. There. Took care of business for today. Except for actually mailing. Maybe I should save mailing it to give me something to do after lunch. I got up and looked out the window some more. I hadn't worked out since the day before I went to New York. I felt tired and heavy. It was six hours until Susan got off work. I could leave the office, mail my letter, have lunch and take a nap until supper time. Or maybe put my laundry through and watch it dry. Time never weighs heavy on the active mind.

There was some mail accumulated at my apartment on Marlborough Street, but except for a letter from Paul Giacomin, it was of less significance than the stuff at my office.

I read Paul's letter, and unpacked my bag, and changed into some sweats and went out to run along the river. I didn't want to and as I started I felt like there was sand in the gears, but as I kept moving things began to loosen in the vernal warmth along the esplanade. A lot of

Frisbee was being played. Some of it with dogs. I had previously observed that dogs who catch Frisbees wear red handkerchiefs instead of dog collars; the accuracy of that observation was once again confirmed. Nothing like investigative training. I ran up to the Mass. Ave. Bridge and across it and down along Memorial Drive and across the old Charles River Dam and back across to Boston. By the time I had run a mile I was loosened up and able to pick up the pace and by the time I got to Leverett Circle I was pounding hard and steady and my shirt was soaking wet. I worked my way through traffic down along the waterfront and went into the Harbor Health Club. I didn't feel like pumping iron, either, but if I didn't rescue what was left after laying off in New York, I would feel even less like it tomorrow. And soon it would be too late.

Henry Cimoli, who ran the place, was taking a young woman through the Nautilus equipment. He had a chart on a clipboard. He wore blue warm-up pants and a white sleeveless T-shirt and white basketball sneakers with padded high tops. There was scar tissue around his eyes and his nose was thickened, and there was a little gray in his short dark hair. But his waist was as narrow and his biceps as thick as when he'd been a featherweight boxer and gone a ten-round draw once with Sandy Saddler.

"Slow," he said to the woman. "It's not how much you do, it's how right you do it."

The woman had on dark blue shiny leotards and pale blue leg warmers and dark blue sneakers with a light blue stripe and a bright blue shiny ribbon tying her hair in a ponytail. She pressed up what appeared to be about forty pounds. I said hello to Henry as I went past. He nodded.

"Now let it back down slow," he said. "Slow, slow."

I started at one end of the Nautilus setup and did three sets of everything. There weren't many people there in midafternoon and I could move from one machine to the next without waiting. I was halfway through when the young lady in the shiny leotard finished working out and headed for the juice bar. Henry stopped to talk.

"Women are good," he said. "They'll do what you tell them and they'll do it strict, get more out of it than the guys. Guys want to pile on too much weight and heave it up, case somebody's watching. So they cheat all the time."

I was doing curls, and it took most of my concentration.

"But women don't know how to try as hard," Henry said. "They do the exercise right but they never learn to strain, you know. The guys do it wrong but will bust their ass doing it."

I finished the fifteenth curl out of the third set. I was breathing hard, getting oxygen in.

"You're not bad," Henry said.

I nodded, getting more air. "Everyone says that," I said.

"Not everybody," Henry said.

I walked back home and showered and changed and had a beer. The first beer after a big workout makes the workout worthwhile. It was a little after four. I called Susan's number and left a message on her machine proposing dinner and talk. She called me back in twenty minutes.

"I have one more patient," she said. "Shall I come there?"

"Yes," I said. "I'll chill the wine."

"Good."

She hung up. I checked my watch. Time to provision. I had a couple of bottles of champagne. I put one in the refrigerator to chill and went to the market.

By six o'clock I was ready. The champagne chilled in a crystal bucket. The boneless chicken was marinating in the juice of one lemon and one orange with a little ginger. The endive and avocado salad was ready to be tossed with dressing and the cornmeal and onion fritters were formed and ready for the skillet. I had on a new starched pink shirt and freshly ironed jeans, and cordovan loafers gleaming with polish. I smelled of cologne. My teeth were brushed and I was more scrumptious than the Dukes of Hazzard.

I was making the salad dressing out of lemon juice and olive oil and honey and mustard and raspberry vinegar when Susan unlocked my front door and came into the apartment. She was wearing a black skirt and a lemon-yellow blouse with black polka dots and a pearl-gray jacket. Her necklace was crystal and pearl, large beads. She wore clunky black earrings and a big bracelet of black and gray chunks of something. Her stockings were pale gray and had a small random floral pattern. Her shoes were black and white. She had her large black purse and a lavender overnight bag.

I watched her come in and take the key out of the lock and store it back in her purse and close the door behind her. I watched while reality rearranged itself so that she formed its center, and I felt my breath go in and out more clearly, as if the air had turned to oxygen.

"You're like a breath of spring," I said. "A whole new thing has happened."

She put her purse down and her overnight bag, and smiled at me and said, "Shall I undress right here, or would you like to sip champagne and talk of the Big Apple, first?"

"Undressing is good," I said.

"Fine," she said, and began to unbutton her jacket. "Feel free to whistle 'Night Train.' "

"Whistling is a little beyond me right now," I said. "Maybe I should just undress."

"Race you," she said.

Then she was naked, wearing only the ankle chain that she always wore because I'd given it to her when we came back from Idaho last year. And we were hugging one another and then we were on the couch.

"How was New York," she said very softly, her lips moving against mine.

"Helluva town," I murmured. "The Bronx is up and the Battery's down."

"You seem very like The Bronx," she said, and pressed her mouth against mine and we didn't talk much for a while.

12

"So," Susan said, "what progress with April?"

We were still undressed, but we were sitting upright on the sofa now, drinking Chandon Blanc de Noirs from fluted glasses, our feet on the coffee table.

"Around none," I said. "There's something I don't like going on, but I don't know what it is."

"You must be used to that by now," Susan said. She had her head resting against my shoulder. My left arm was around her.

"I've never learned to like it," I said. "I go see April and then when I go back she's gone, so I go see her pimp and somebody has obviously cleaned his clock and he won't say anything and he's scared to death and says I'm going to get us both killed. So I leave him and go see Ginger Buckey and she's not on the streets."

"Maybe the women are simply busy at their work."

"Maybe. But who beat up Rambeaux and why and what have I got to do with it?"

"You're sure it was because of you?"

"Yeah. Rambeaux was clear on that. His biggest sweat

was to get me out of there and not be seen with me. He was so scared he couldn't sit straight."

Susan was tracing the mark on my chest where Sherry Spellman had shot me. Low down there was another mark and below that a mark where there had been a drain.

"God," Susan said, "you look like a scuffed shoe."

"But sinewy and desirable," I said.

"Of course." She sipped some champagne and leaned forward and got the bottle out of the ice bucket and poured some in her glass and poured some in my glass.

"What are you going to do now?" she said.

"I'll call Ginger Buckey," I said. "See if she knows anything about where April went."

"Why should she know?"

"It's not that she should," I said. "It's simply that she's all I have."

"And if she doesn't know?"

I shrugged and drank some champagne and my doorbell rang.

"We could ignore it," Susan said.

I shook my head. Susan smiled.

"Of course we can't," she said. "It might be an orphan of the storm seeking shelter."

I got my pants on and took my gun off the counter and buzzed the caller in and looked through the peephole in the door. In a moment Frank Belson appeared on the other side.

"Balls," I said, and put the gun back on the counter.

"Balls?" Susan said.

"Frank Belson," I said. "I gotta let him in."

"Of course," Susan said, and got up and went into my bedroom and closed the door. I opened the front door and Belson came in. He glanced at Susan's clothing in a small pile on the living room floor and didn't change expression.

"You want some champagne?" I said.

"What else you got?" Belson said. He wore his summer straw with the big blue band and his seersucker suit, very recently pressed.

"Got some Black Bush a guy brought back to me from Ireland," I said.

His thin face softened slightly. He nodded. I went to the kitchen and poured the whiskey neat into a lowball glass and handed it to him. He took a sip and tipped his head back and let it slide down his throat. He smiled in a satisfied way.

"New York cops want to talk with you," he said.

"They looking for crime-stopper tips?" I said.

He shook his head and sipped the whiskey again. "They found a dead hooker with your card in her purse."

"Shit," I said.

"You know her?"

"Ginger Buckey," I said.

Belson nodded. "Detective second grade named Corsetti caught the squeal, found the card, called us to see if we knew you."

"She murdered?"

"You think they're going to call us on somebody hit by a cab in Queens?"

"No. How was she killed?"

"Gunshot, Corsetti didn't say much."

"Am I a suspect?"

Belson shook his head. "Naw, they just want to know if you got anything would help. I told them I knew you, I'd swing by and ask."

"I was looking for another whore, kid named April Kyle. Ginger Buckey had the same pimp and I asked her if she knew about April and she said no."

"What's the pimp's name?"

"Rambeaux," I said. "Robert Rambeaux, lives on Seventy-seventh Street." I gave him the number.

"Any thoughts on who done it?"

"No, but it's sour," I said. "I found April and then she disappeared. So I went to see Rambeaux and somebody had beat him up and scared him gray. He said I was going to get him killed. Then I went to ask Ginger Buckey some more questions and I couldn't find her and now she's dead."

"Anything else?" Belson said. He walked to my kitchen and poured another shot of whiskey.

"April worked out of a house called Tiger Lilies."

"Elegant," Belson said. He drank some whiskey and shook his head with respect.

"New York ain't going to put people on overtime," he said. "Hookers get aced, you know."

"Tell them to check Rambeaux," I said.

"Sure," Belson said. "They sit around waiting for me to call and tell them what to do. They're grateful as hell when I do."

"Drink the Black Bush," I said.

"Sure, but not fast. It's a waste to drink it fast."

"Take the glass," I said. "Sip it in the car."

Belson grinned for the first time. "Okay," he said. He glanced at the tangle of clothes on the floor. "My love to Susan," he said.

13

Maine is much bigger than any of the other New England states and large stretches of it are, to put it kindly, rural. Lindell is more rural than most of Maine. If three people left, it would be more rural than the moon. The center of town appeared around a curve in a road that ran through scrub forest. There was a cinder block store with a green translucent plastic portico in front and two gas pumps. Next to it was a gray-shingled bungalow with a white sign out front that said in black letters LINDELL, MAINE, and below it U.S. POST OFFICE. Across the street was a bowling alley with a sign in the window that said *Coors* in red neon script. Beyond the three buildings the road continued its curve back into the scrub forest.

Some years back there had been a timbering industry, but when the forest got depleted, the timber companies moved on while Lindell sat around and waited for the new trees to grow. I parked in front of the Lindell sign and went into the building. Half of it was post office, one window and a bank of post office boxes along the wall. The other half of the building was the site of town government in Lindell. Town government appeared to be a fat woman in a shapeless dress sitting at a yellow pine table with two file cabinets behind her. I smiled at her. She nodded.

"Hello," I said. "I'm looking for a man named Vern Buckey."

The fat woman said, "Why?"

"I need to talk with him about his daughter."

"Vern don't like to talk to people," the woman said. There was a gap in her upper front teeth about four teeth wide.

I smiled at her again. She didn't swoon. Was I losing it? Of course not. She was just obdurate.

"Sure, ma'am. I don't blame him. I respect a person's privacy. But this might be important to Vern." If the smile didn't work, the silver tongue would.

"Vern don't like people talking about him neither," she said.

"Well, sure," I said. I was smiling and talking. "Nobody does, but why don't you just tell me where he is and I'm sure I can explain it to him."

"Vern don't like people telling other people where he lives."

"Lady," I said, "I don't actually give a rat's ass what Vern likes, if you really want to know. I drove seven hours to talk with him and I want to know where he is."

The woman laughed a wheezy laugh. "A rat's ass," she said, and laughed some more. "By God."

She fumbled around in the litter on the table and found a tired-looking pack of Camels and got one out and lit it with a kitchen match that she scratched on the underside of the table. She inhaled some smoke and blew it out with a kind of snort.

"Well," she said, "you're a pretty good-sized fella."

"But fun-loving," I said, "and kind to my mother."

She smoked some more of her Camel. "Let me tell you something for your own good," she said. She was squinting through the smoke from the cigarette, which she left in the corner of her mouth while she talked. "If you go bothering Vern Buckey he'll knock you down and kick you like a dog."

"Even if I object?"

She laughed again, wheezing, and choked a little on the smoke of her cigarette and laughed and choked and wheezed at the same time.

"Object," she gasped. "You can object like a . . . like a rat's ass," and she laughed and wheezed so hard she couldn't talk for a minute. She stopped laughing and wheezed a little longer and got her breath back and squinted at me some more.

"You are a by-God big one," she said. "Might be sorta interesting."

I was gaining ground, so I shut up and smiled and listened. Susan said it was a technique I might consider polishing.

The fat woman pointed with her chin. "Vern's truck is parked 'cross the street in front of the bowling alley. He'll be inside drinking beer."

"Thank you," I said.

She inhaled, coughed, and chuckled in her wheezy way. "Rat's ass," she said.

I was wearing jeans and running shoes and a gray sleeveless T-shirt and a gray silk tweed summer jacket and a gun. I took off the jacket, and unclipped the gun from my belt and folded the jacket on top of the gun and put them on the front seat of my car. Then I walked across the street and into the bowling alley. The bowling alley was one of those round-topped corrugated buildings that look like a big Quonset hut or a small airplane hangar. There were only three lanes inside, and a snack bar that sold beer and sandwiches. No one was bowling. A short dark-haired man with a bald spot and tattooed arms was behind the bar. He had on a sleeveless undershirt with a spot of ketchup on it. Sitting on a barstool drinking Budweiser beer from a long-necked bottle was a guy with a round red face and a big hard belly. He was entirely bald and his head seemed to swell out of his thick shoulders without benefit of neck. He had small piggy eyes under scant eyebrows that were blond or white and barely visible and his thick flared short nose looked like a snout. The eyes and nose gave his face a swinish cast. He was wearing a dirty white T-shirt and baggy blue overalls and work boots. He hadn't shaved recently, but his beard, like his eyebrows, was so pale that it only gave a shabby glint to his red skin. He wasn't talking to the bartender, and he wasn't looking at the soap opera on television. He was staring straight ahead and drinking the beer. When I came in he shifted his stare at me and in its meanness it was nearly tangible. The hand wrapped around the beer bottle was thick and hammy with big knuckles. There was no air-conditioning in the place but a big floor fan hummed near the bar, pushing the hot air around the dim room.

I said, "Vern Buckey?"

He unhooked his bootheels from the lower rung of the barstool and let his feet drop to the floor and stood up. He was at least six feet four, which gave him three inches on me, and he must have weighed eighty pounds more than my two hundred. A lot of it was stomach but what he lacked in conditioning he probably made up in meanness.

"What did you say?" He spoke in a hoarse kind of whisper.

"Vern Buckey."

"I don't like you saying that," he rasped.

"I don't blame you," I said. "Sounds like an asshole

name to me, too, but I want to talk with you about your daughter."

Buckey put the beer bottle down on the counter and stepped toward me.

"Get the fuck out of here," he said.

"Your daughter's dead," I said.

"I told you to get out," he said, and took another step. "People round here do what I say."

"I need to know about Ginger, Vern."

"Then I'm going to rack your ass," he said.

I shrugged. "Sure. In the parking lot. No point messing up this slick amusement complex."

I turned and went out the door. In the parking lot cars and pickup trucks and two motorcycles had arrived. People sat in the cars and trucks and on the bikes in a kind of expectant semicircle. The fat woman from the town office was there with a group of other citizens in a cluster, near Buckey's green Ford truck. I gave her a short thumbs-up gesture. She poked an elbow into the man next to her and pointed at me with her chin. I could hear her wheeze. Buckey came out of the bowling alley squinting with his little pig eyes in the glare of the summer. He looked around at the circle of onlookers and hunched his shoulders as if to get a kink out and came straight at me.

"Talked with a sheriff's deputy on the phone before I

came up," I said. "Said you were crazy. Said everyone in this part of the state was afraid of you."

Bucky tried to kick me in the groin and I turned and he missed and grunted and turned toward me again.

"Said even the cops are afraid of you because you're nuts." He kicked at me again and missed again. I was moving around him. He was massive and relentless but he wasn't very fast. If I didn't let my mind wander, I could probably avoid him. It was why I'd come out. I didn't want the fight confined in a small space.

"Said you'd get on someone's case and maybe they'd be driving along at night and someone would backshoot them with a deer rifle at an intersection."

Buckey rushed at me and I slipped aside and slapped him across the face. The sound of it made several onlookers gasp.

"They know it's you but they can't catch you."

Buckey hit me a roundhouse right-hand punch on the upper left arm and numbness set in at once. He followed with a left but I rolled away from it.

"I can see why you're a backshooter, Vern," I said. "You can't hit shit with your fists."

Buckey was a little quicker than he looked and got hold of my shirtfront, and as I tried to yank away he hit me with his right hand again, this time on the side of my head just in front of my left ear. Bells rang. I brought both fists down on his hand where it held my shirt. I didn't loosen his grip, but the shirt tore and I pulled away.

"Best punch you've got, Vern?"

He kept coming. I don't even know if he heard my chatter. His eyes pinched nearly shut. His face a fiery red, sweat running down his cheeks, a froth of saliva at the corner of his mouth, he kept at me like a Cape buffalo: stupid, implacable, brutish and mad.

Fighting is hard work. Big as he was and mean as he was, Buckey was not in training. Most of his fights were one- or two-punch affairs. Knock the victim down and then kick him awhile. Not taxing, except on the kickee. But Vern was having trouble getting me to stay still and in a while he was going to get tired. It wasn't going to be a very long while. I stepped in quick, smacked Buckey on the snout, and moved back away. Blood started down over his lips and chin. He rubbed the back of his left hand over his mouth and looked at the smear of blood and made a sort of growl and rushed at me. I spun aside and kicked him on the side of the left knee and it buckled under him and he went down. Behind me I heard a man say, "Jesus Christ."

Buckey scrambled to his feet. He limped slightly on the knee I'd kicked and he moved more slowly. The blood from his nose was reddening his T-shirt, mixing with the sweat that had already soaked it. Where he'd fallen some of the parking lot gravel stuck to the moisture. He was breathing hard. He lunged at me again and threw a handful of gravel at my face. It didn't have much effect. But it distracted me for half a second and Vern hit me on the left side of the jaw and knocked me two staggering steps and down flat on my back. My head echoed with hollow distance and my vision blurred. He jumped through the blur, kicking at my head, and, mostly on instinct, I half rolled and got my hands up and the kick hit my upper arm. I kept rolling and crab-scrambled away from the next kick and got my feet under me and was up. I felt dizzy. Vern hit me again on the upper left arm, and then on the right forearm as I covered up and deflected the punches. The ringing in my head was clearing. I could hear Vern's breath rasping in and out. He tried to get his arms around me in a bear hug and when he did I kneed him in the groin and butted him under the chin and broke away. He was gasping and shaking his head, half doubled over in pain. But his eyes were fixed on me with the same red intensity they had when he stepped out of the bowling alley. He was drooling a little and bleeding and soaked with sweat and filthy with dust and gravel. He was breathing like a bellows, oxygen heaving into his chest. But he had stopped coming at me. He stood still, swaying slightly, his head shaking slightly.

"Vern," I said, "you're just not in shape." I shook my head. "Shame to see a man let himself go like this."

He came at me again, but more slowly. Not cautiously, but in a slower-motion version of the way he had come at me before. There was no change in expression. I made a little feint with my left hand and hooked it over his shoulder and got him on the jaw. I moved away from his punch and hit him a combination, left, left, overhand right. And moved away. Vern turned slowly toward me. His arms were starting to drop. It was what I used to look for when I was fighting. Your opponent got arm-weary and he let them drop and you went for his head. I hit Vern another combination. My head was clear now and the oxygen was flowing in and out easily and the legs were good and the muscles were loose and I could see very clearly. I could see the openings where the punches could go and I was moving in the clean, precise automatic sequences I had learned a long time ago when I thought I was going to be heavyweight champ. Vern was pushing his punches at me now. It was almost done. I knew there were people watching and I knew the sun was out but none of that had any reality, only the swaying massive shape in front of me and the punching lanes and the sequenced movements. It was like dancing to music only I could hear. Even Vern barely mattered in the intensity of my concentration and the rhythms of the fight. There was no pain. Later there would be, but not now. Just the patterns and the movements and the solid jolt as the punches landed.

And then he was through.

He didn't go down. But his arms dropped; he stopped coming, even slowly, and stood motionless, his arms down, gasping for air. I stepped back away from him. The intensity was gone. The meanness was gone. In his eyes there was nothing. As if all he was was mean and if he lost it he ceased to exist. Around us most of the people north of Bangor stood in a ragged semicircle in absolute silence. I could hear my breathing deep and steady easing in and out, and I could hear Buckey rasping desperately. Somewhere in the scrub forests along the highway some kind of bird was making a persistent sound like chips being sliced from a hardwood slab.

Behind me a man's voice said, "Put him away, mister."

And another voice, male also: "Put him down, man. . . . Put the sonova bitch down."

I said to Buckey, "You ready to talk about Ginger?"

A woman's voice said, "Knock him down, mister."

And a man said, "Don't stop until it's done."

A lot of voices chimed in. Vern wasn't only disliked. He was disliked widely.

A woman said, "Kill the bastard."

Buckey still stood motionless, still swaying slightly,

his head down, gasping. Then he slowly bent forward and his knees buckled and he fell like a weed wilting, crumpling to the ground and lying still with his face in the gravel. Again there was silence and then someone began to clap and then the odd rural crowd began to applaud steadily.

Now I was the toughest guy in Lindell, Maine.

14

Buckey's pulse was strong and I propped him in the shade against the east wall of the bowling alley. The bartender with the tattoos brought me a bucket of water and some ice and a rag and I sponged Buckey off and soaked my hands and waited. I was sitting on my heels with both hands in the ice-water bucket when Buckey opened his eyes.

I didn't move. His eyes slowly focused on me. I put the ice bucket aside and rested my forearms on my thighs and folded my hands. His eyes moved past me. There was no one else. The big fight was over. The audience had gone away. He looked back at me.

"I'm going to kill you," he said.

I nodded.

"When you're sleeping or getting laid or walking along not thinking about it, I'm going to be there and blow the back of your fucking head away."

I nodded again. I had my gun back on my belt and sitting still on my heels I reached around with my right hand and took it out and pointed it at the tip of Buckey's nose and said, "Maybe."

Buckey looked at the muzzle of the gun two inches from his face. He didn't say anything.

I said, "Now I want you to tell me about your daughter, Ginger."

"I ain't telling you fucking shit," he said. But it was weak.

"You've been doing that," I said. "And look what it got you. I want to know about the whorehouse you sold your kid to."

"She's dead," he said.

"Yeah, she was a street hooker in New York City and somebody shot her."

"So what's the fucking difference?" Buckey said.

"Fatherhood rests but lightly on you, Vern," I said. And I thumbed the hammer back on my gun. It made the cylinder turn one notch and Vern could see the copper-jacketed slug go under the hammer. "What whorehouse?"

Buckey shrugged. "Place called Magic Massage in Portland. I didn't sell her. It was a finder's fee."

"Place still there?" I said.

"Was last time I was down to Portland, on Congress Street, around the corner from Franklin."

I smiled, and turned the gun away from his face and let the hammer down gently. Then I flipped the cylinder out, turned it so there was an empty chamber under the hammer, closed the gun and put it back on my hip. Vern watched me.

"You had a fucking gun why didn't you use it," he said. "How come you come on to me without it, if you had one?"

"Wanted to see if you really were the toughest guy in Lindell," I said. I stood up. "See you around, Vern."

"That's all?" Buckey said. "You come up here all this way to fight me and find out about a whorehouse in Portland?"

"Un huh."

"You're fucking crazy, man. What do you care about a whorehouse in Portland? What the fuck you care about some dead whore in New York?"

"Vern," I said, "it was a pleasure to punch your lights out. It was such a pleasure that I may come up sometime and do it again."

I turned and left him sitting slumped against the wall and headed for my car and drove away, back south. Toward Portland.

15

The sky over Portland is like the sky above San Francisco, unusually blue and high, suggestive of the ocean that surrounds the city on most sides. The buildings were low and that emphasized the high of the sky and the silent presence of the ocean.

I parked along the restored waterfront on Commercial Street and walked up through the Old Port Exchange area to Congress Street. The Old Port Exchange was urban renewal at its chichiest. The nineteenth-century granite buildings restored and full of restaurants and dress shops and places with names like The Elegant Elephant. The people walking about in the area could have been from Boston or Chicago. It was startling when they spoke in the Titus Moody accent that had persisted even here among the bleached oak and hanging plants.

I passed a shop called Gazelle, and a bookstore that displayed the complete works of Thomas Merton in the window, and turned east on Congress Street. The Holiday Inn where I'd spent the night had a map of downtown Portland in its lobby and I had spent a minute in front of it after breakfast. Like Boston, Portland was a red-brick city. There were occasional granite and brownstone buildings and the usual ugly newer ones, but mostly it was red brick. Past Franklin Street, at the east end of Portland, the Magic Massage Parlor, Massages by Women, stood across the street from a store that sold scuba gear.

The storefront display windows were discreetly curtained on the first floor, but a small card in the lower left-hand corner of the biggest window said OPEN. I crossed the street and leaned against the front wall of the dive shop and scoped things out.

Magic Massage was in a three-story brick building. In addition to the massage parlor entrance there was another door. A sign in gilt lettering on the door said LONGFELLOW HOUSE, ROOMS. The two floors above the massage parlor had small balconies. The trim was neatly painted white. The neighborhood was good, the place was neat. Looked like a better deal than Lindell. A brown Chevy van went by with a couple of Cumberland County sheriff's deputies in it. They paid no attention to me or Magic Massage. I shifted position a little and felt the stiffness from yesterday's fight. I looked at myself in the window of the dive shop. The left side of my face was puffy. I hadn't shaved this morning to spare the puffiness and I had a small dark stubble beginning to show. I looked sort of sinister.

Across the street a customer appeared at Magic Massage. He had a crew cut. He wore a red-and-white-striped short-sleeved knit shirt that was stretched tight over his bulging stomach. He had on new jeans with the bottoms rolled a couple of turns to feature his new shiny brown shoes with three lace-eyelets and thick soles. Nineteen fifty-two grown old. He opened the door with the confidence of an old customer and went in and closed it behind him.

I flexed my hands. They were sore and stiff and the knuckles were swollen. Maybe I should rely more on sweet reason.

I crossed Congress Street again and went in the door of Magic Massage. A small sticker above the doorknob said that MasterCard and Visa were welcome. Inside there was a short high counter to the right. A middle-aged woman with purplish red hair sat behind it. There was a cash register on the counter, and a phone, and one of those little devices that take a credit card imprint. The room was small. Against the far wall was a sofa covered in tan Naugahyde. The arms and legs were dark oak. There were two matching chairs against the left wall and a low coffee table with an assortment of magazines. In the angle of the wall opposite the counter a small color-television set was showing a talk show in which the host and audience were debating sex-change operations with an intensity that suggested almost everyone might have one.

Leaning against the end of the counter was a tall guy wearing a beige gaberdine suit and black cowboy boots. He had on a white shirt and wore one of those odd little shoestring pieces of neckware fastened at the throat with a silver clasp. On his head was a big black cowboy hat with the brim turned down all the way. His face was thin and he had a long pointy nose and prominent upper teeth and a large Adam's apple. His hands were big and the knuckles were outsized. He wore a big ring with a blue stone in it on his little finger, left hand. There was a thin, jagged-looking scar along his jawline almost back to his left ear that looked as if someone had tried to cut his throat with a broken bottle five or ten years ago and made the swipe too high.

The woman said, "A nice massage today, sir?" She had on a red blouse and wore big round rose-tinted glasses with blue frames, the kind where the bows come off the bottom instead of the top.

I said, "This is sort of embarrassing, but may I speak to the manager?"

The tall guy in the cowboy hat said, "What do you want to see the manager about?" He was looking very hard at me. Hard enough to notice that someone had whacked me recently along the side of the head. He seemed like a man who noticed such things.

"I'd like to ask about a young woman," I said, "used to work here."

"You ain't a cop," he said.

"I'm too polite," I said.

"Un huh."

"I'm working on a thing in New York," I said. "No problem for you."

"Private cop," he said.

"Yes."

"There a reward?"

"No," I said, "except I go away and don't annoy you."

He nodded. "What's her name?" he said.

"You the manager?" I said.

He grinned. His bottom teeth were missing in front. "I represent the manager," he said. "What's her name?"

"Ginger Buckey."

A guy in a gray plaid suit came in. He looked at us uneasily. The tall guy gestured with his head and we walked over to a door beyond the sofa. Behind me I heard the lady with the purplish red hair say, "A nice massage today?"

We went through the door and into a corridor. There was a stairwell up the right wall. The tall guy opened one of the doors. It was a small room like the examining room at a doctor's office. The walls were narrow vertical planking painted green. There was a table covered with a white sheet, a straight chair, and a small side table with baby oil and lilac water and a small pile of towels on it. The tall guy closed the door and leaned against it.

"Customers get sort of nervous they see a guy looks like you hanging around in the reception area."

"Afraid I'm a cop?"

"Well, you got the look, 'cept you're so polite."

"Nothing wrong with a good massage," I said. "No law against that."

"Sure, what do you want to know about Ginger Buckey?"

"Where she went from here," I said.

"Beats me," he said.

"Her father brought her to you," I said, "and you gave him a finder's fee. Now that may be doing business just like U.S. Steel does business, but it might be white slavery."

"And if it was?"

"If it was, or if it looked like it was, I bet I could get the cops and Cumberland County and maybe the U.S. Attorney's office interested enough in whether it was white slavery or not to make a genuine economic impact on the business here."

"Maybe you'd end up feeding lobsters in Casco Bay, you did that," he said.

"Tough talk for a guy wearing a shoestring for a tie," I said. "I'm already the toughest guy in Lindell."

"Where the fuck is Lindell?" he said.

"It's where Ginger came from. Why do this hard? You tell me where she went from here and I go away and leave you to massage your way to health and fortune, maybe even get yourself a lower plate. You don't, and either you've got to put me in the bay, which I don't think you can do, or have me accusing you of trafficking in children. The *Press Herald* will be on your ass, and the cops. It'll be awful."

He was wearing a gun under his left arm. You can wear a gun without it showing, but some guys want it to show, and some guys don't care.

"You don't think I can handle you," he said.

"If I thought you could, would I still be here annoying you?"

He put his left hand into his side pocket and came out with a pair of brass knuckles. He put them on his right hand and moved it in a little circle at waist level and said, "Now what do you think?"

I sighed. "I think it's been a hard year," I said. "And I'm tired. And I think you are dumb as hell to put those things on your right hand, which means it will take you an hour and ten minutes to get your gun out from under your left arm, whereas I . . ." I took the gun off my hip and showed it to him without really pointing it. He looked at the gun. His right fist stopped moving in a circle.

I said, "Sort of embarrassing, huh?"

He let his fist drop to his side. "Now what?" he said.

"I don't feel like shooting you," I said. "I don't feel like taking your brass knuckles away and knocking you down and kicking out the rest of your teeth. All I want is to leave you in peace and good health and go see the people that Ginger Buckey left you for."

"I'll get in trouble," he said.

"They won't know," I said.

"How do I know you won't tell them?"

"Because I said I wouldn't."

"And if I don't tell you?"

"I blow the whistle on this place so loud that the people you're bribing won't be able to help, and the ownership will get in trouble and be mad as hell at you."

"For crissake, man, she was already a pro when we got her."

"She was fourteen," I said. "White slavery, babe. Film at eleven."

"I passed her on to a guy from Boston," he said.

"Who?"

"Guy named Art Floyd."

"And what did he do with her?" I was still holding

the gun in a sort of random way, not exactly pointing but not really hanging at my side either.

"How the fuck do I know, man. Probably put her in a house up there. You think we had a long talk about it?"

"Did Ginger want to go?"

The tall guy laughed. "Something else we didn't have a long talk about."

"Finder's fee," I said.

"Sure," he said. "She's product, man. You know? You raise cattle, you give the cows away?"

"So you sold her to a guy from Boston named Art Floyd."

"Yeah."

"Okay," I said. "I'll see if I can locate Art. If I can't I'll come back."

"Hey, man, he said he was from Boston. What can I tell you?"

I nodded. "Give me your gun," I said. I leveled my gun as he took his knuckles off and put them in his pocket again and took a Browning automatic out of his shoulder holster and handed it to me.

"Cost me $475," he said.

"I'll give it to you outside," I said. "I just don't want you shooting me while I walk away."

"I wouldn't backshoot you, man."

"Course you wouldn't," I said, and went out of the

room and through the reception area. The tall guy followed me. The threat of him was gone. He wanted his gun back. I got in my car and opened the window. I took the clip out of the gun and checked the action once to make sure there was nothing in the chamber. I thumbed the bullets out of the clip. Put the clip back in the gun and handed it to him.

"You gonna keep the bullets?" he said.

"Oh, hell," I said, and put my hand out. He cupped his hand and I let the bullets fall into it.

"You won't tell Floyd, will you?" he said.

"No," I said, "I won't."

16

The only Arthur Floyd in the Boston phone book was a retired pediatrician. It didn't prove he wasn't a whorehouse recruiter, but it cut down on the probability enough for me to look elsewhere.

I called a vice squad cop named McNeeley. He had never heard of Arthur Floyd. It was possible that the cowboy in Portland had been jiving me, but I didn't think so. He had been so worried about getting his gun back that he'd have told on his mother.

Just because Arthur Floyd wasn't in the Boston phone book didn't mean he wasn't around. He might be in the Worcester phone book, or Lynn, or Fall River. Or Tucson or Detroit. I had a lot of options. If I went through every phone book for every city in the country, I'd be sure to find him. Unless he had an unpublished number. Or had moved to Toronto. I could open my office window and shout down at the people going by on Berkeley Street, and ask them if they knew anyone named Arthur Floyd. Maybe I should just ask for Floyd, since Art might be a nickname. On the other hand Floyd might be an alias.

Maybe I should just yell down and ask if they knew anyone. Or maybe I should go work out.

I chose the last course and went down to the Harbor Health Club. When I had begun working out there, the Harbor Health Club had been appropriate to the waterfront. As the waterfront went upscale so did the Harbor Health Club. Only Henry Cimoli's influence kept the boxing room from being turned into a boutique. There was one speed bag, one heavy bag, and a jump rope pressed into a narrow corner by the steady spread of steam rooms and sauna and eucalyptus inhalant rooms and sun-tanning rooms and juice bars and a heated pool and an overgrowth of hanging plants that made the place look like a Henri Rousseau painting. Hawk was there to add to the illusion. His shaved black head gleamed among the potted ferns as he walked toward the Nautilus room. He was wearing a magenta tank top and white satin warm-up pants and a white terry sweatband with a thin magenta stripe in it.

"Christ," I said. "Designer sweats."

Hawk grinned. "Clothes make the man, babe."

"Don't people call you a sissy when they see you dressed like that?"

Hawk's grin widened slightly. "No," he said. He took the handles at the pull-up station and began to do pull-ups with his legs held parallel to the ground. The muscles in his arms and shoulders swelled and relaxed as he went up and down as if they were separately alive. People, as they always did, peeked at him when they thought he wasn't looking, glancing out of the corners of eyes and in reflections in the glass. Hawk knew it. He always knew everything that went on around him. It made no impression on him. Almost nothing did. He didn't enjoy it. He didn't mind it.

I was doing curls. Hawk said, "How you and Susan doing?"

"Love is lovelier," I said, "the second time around."

"Worth the scramble," Hawk said.

"Yes."

Hawk shifted from pull-ups to dips. He whistled to himself through his teeth, his lips together so one barely heard the small internal melody. He was whistling "On the Atchison, Topeka and Santa Fe." We both finished on the Nautilus equipment and went to the boxing room. I jumped rope, Hawk played games on the speed bag. Now he was whistling "Sweet Georgia Brown."

I said, "You still on good terms with Tony Marcus?"

Hawk said, "Sure."

I said, "I think I need some help from him."

"Nothing Tony like better," Hawk said, "than to do favors for some honkie who punched him in the mouth the only time he met him."

"It's why I asked about your terms," I said. "If he liked me I wouldn't need you."

"If you need me 'cause people don't like you, babe, you need me bad. What you want from Tony?"

I crossed and uncrossed the rope as I jumped. "I'm looking for a guy named Art Floyd. He recruited a kid for a whorehouse in Boston."

"You looking for the kid?"

"No. I'm looking for him. The kid's dead."

"Well, Tony the man," Hawk said. "Nothing much happens in the whore business that Tony don't follow. Floyd kill the kid?"

"No, I doubt it. I'm looking for April Kyle again."

"The little blond kid from Smithfield."

"Un huh."

"Man," Hawk said, "you do hang in there. Tell me about it, maybe we work something out with Tony."

I told him about April and about Ginger Buckey.

"So you figure you find out what happened to Ginger Buckey you maybe find out what happened to April," Hawk said.

"April's gone, Ginger's dead, and Rambeaux is scared. There's got to be a connection."

"Well, I see what I can do. But Tony don't remember you fondly."

"I'm not asking him to dance."

"Good to know," Hawk said. "What Tony get out of this?"

I shrugged. "A favor to me?"

"Besides that," Hawk said.

"A favor to you?"

"Tony usually looking to get favors more than he looking to give them," Hawk said.

"Okay, we'll owe him one," I said.

"What this 'we' shit, white man?"

17

Hawk and I met Tony Marcus at a Chinese restaurant called Ming Garden on Route 9 across from the Chestnut Hill Mall. Marcus was maybe my age with a modified Afro and a thick mustache. The mustache had some gray in it, but his face was smooth and unlined. He sat in a booth alone toward the far end of the restaurant. At a table next to him four other black men sat with menus closed in front of them. All of them wore suits. One of the guys sitting with his back toward us was too heavy for the suit and where it pulled tight across his back I could see the faint line of a shoulder-holster strap.

"Why here?" I said to Hawk as we walked toward them.

Hawk shrugged. "Likes the food, I guess. Man was willing to come, I didn't ask many questions."

We reached the booth. Marcus smiled. The four guys at the table all looked at us without any expressions. Marcus gestured that we should sit across from him and we did. Hawk slid in first and I sat beside him.

"Tony," I said.

"Good Szechwan cooking," Marcus said. "You like Szechwan, this is the place. Better than Chinatown."

I nodded. A waiter showed up with some Chinese beer and put it down and went away. "I already ordered," Marcus said.

"Thoughtful," I said.

The waiter returned with two platters of Peking ravioli and some hoisin sauce. Marcus smiled again, and rubbed his hands softly together. We each ate a ravioli and drank some beer. The four guys at the next table weren't eating or drinking. They just sat.

"Understand you looking for a man," Marcus said.

"Art Floyd," I said.

Marcus nodded.

"You know him?" I said.

Marcus nodded again. He speared a second ravioli from the platter and spooned a little sauce over it and cut it in two with the edge of his fork.

"You find him he going to be in trouble?"

"I don't know," I said. "I'm looking for a kid and it depends on how willing he is to help me."

Tony ate half his ravioli. Patted his lips with his napkin, took a sip of Tsingtao beer, and said, "Maybe it ought to depend on whether I want him in trouble or not."

"Do you?" I said.

Marcus smiled again. "Un huh."

I nodded. "That's what you get out of it," I said.

"Un huh."

"What kind of trouble you want him in?"

"What kind you got?" Marcus said.

"Tell me about him," I said. "We can work something out."

The Peking ravioli were gone. The waiter took the platter, replaced it with mu-shu pork and another round of beers.

"Running whores is traditionally black turf," Marcus said. "In New York, in Chicago, in Detroit . . . here." He put a pancake on his plate and added a spoonful of mu-shu and carefully folded it over into a neat package and took a bite. Then he drank some beer and used his napkin. "Been that way a long time and everyone sort of accepts that."

I nodded.

"Which means here it's mine," Marcus said.

"Okay by me," I said.

"Even if it's not," Marcus said.

"Just being polite," I said.

"Polite is shutting up and listening, sowbelly," Marcus said.

I looked at Hawk. "Sowbelly?"

"White," Hawk said, "like salt pork. He insulting you."

"Ahhh," I said.

"Maybe you ought to sit on it too, Hawk," Marcus said. The four guys at the next table all looked over at us. Hawk poured the rest of his second bottle of beer into his glass, tipping the glass slightly so that the head of foam worked just right. He put the empty bottle down, picked up the glass, took a sip, looked for a minute at the color of the beer, holding it so the light showed through. Then he put the glass down and leaned back in the booth and looked at Marcus.

"Ain't enough of you, Tony, to smartmouth both of us," he said.

Marcus looked back at him and then looked away. "Fuck that," he said, and made a dismissive gesture with his hand. "Let's talk business."

Hawk smiled and drank a little more beer. I waited.

"Artic Floyd works for a guy named Perry Lehman. You know Lehman?"

I nodded. "Skin magazines."

"That's one part of it," Marcus said. "Soft porn, hard porn, gay porn, kid porn, fetish porn." Marcus paused and finished his pancake. He made another one. "Lehman got magazines for every taste." The waiter appeared and took away the empty platters and brought a bowl of steamed rice and a platter of chicken with cashews. Marcus gestured at the beer and the waiter went for some. "I think it's shit but no skin off my ass, is it." Marcus spoke in a neutral dialect most of the time, softly, like an FM announcer. But every once in a while there was a Caribbean trace in his speech. He served himself some chicken and some rice. "Then he branches out. He opens a series of resorts and vacation clubs and he starts staffing them with hostesses. At which point he starts cutting into part of my franchise. So I have lunch with him one day, and I tell him that he's off base. And that he should stick to the fuck magazines and let me run the actual fucking." Marcus drank some beer. "Try the chicken," he said. "Stuff's excellent."

I nodded and put a little on my plate.

"So the fucking sleaze bag says, sure. Right. He hadn't realized that, and he'd take care of it, and maybe we could work out . . . what the hell he say . . ." Marcus put his head back for a moment then looked back at me. "A franchising fee. A fucking franchising fee, man." Marcus shook his head. "Shit!"

I ate the chicken. It was good. But I had already had more lunch than I was used to. The beer was good too. Marcus seemed to have a low tolerance for it. As he ate and drank he talked faster and louder and more profanely and the island accent became more frequent.

"So I tell him to go think about it and we'll have lunch next week and we'll come to a decision. And I go and talk to some of my money people and they say maybe some sort of fee isn't a bad move, and I say no, you let the little Hymie prick in, man, and pretty soon he's all the way in."

"And there goes the neighborhood," I said.

Marcus paid no attention. He was rolling. "So I have lunch with him the next week, Jap restaurant in Harvard Square, and he don't show up. Instead a couple of wise guys show up."

"Vinnie Morris?" I said.

Marcus shook his head. "Not Vinnie. This is bigger than Joe Broz. You don't need to know the names."

"Lehman's connected," I said.

"Indeed," Marcus said.

"Connected so good that you can't touch him."

"It's a boat I don't want to rock," Marcus said.

"And you want me to rock it."

Marcus finished another beer and glanced around for the waiter.

"Anything bad happening to Lehman is good happening to me," he said.

The waiter appeared, with more beer. "Never mind the beer," Marcus said. "Gimme a double Scotch."

"Okay," I said. "Let's start with Artie Floyd. I find him and we'll see what happens."

Marcus said, "Daryl?" and the big guy with the telltale shoulder strap said, "He lives in Salem, Six Grey Street, down by the water."

The waiter came back with Marcus's Scotch, and another showed up with littlenecks in black bean sauce. I stood up. Hawk followed.

"Thanks for lunch," I said.

"Don't miss the clams," Marcus said. "Clams are the best."

I shook my head.

Hawk said, "Bon appétit."

And we left the restaurant.

18

The Salem waterfront was in the early throes of restoration chic. Run-down buildings were being rehabbed and condo-ized, people were buying Jeeps and BMWs, the bars were serving nachos and potato skins, there were Vietnamese and Mexican restaurants, and it was only a matter of time before nouvelle cuisine was vying for position with Cajun cooking. Looming over all were the twin stacks of the power plant, which gently dusted the new condos with a fine black grit.

I drove down Derby Street past the Pickering Wharf development, full of restaurants, and shops that sold things like teddy bears and silk flowers, past the old custom house where Hawthorne had worked, past a barroom called In a Pig's Eye, and turned right onto Grey Street behind the House of Seven Gables.

Grey Street was very short and ended in a boatyard. Just before the boatyard was a five-unit condominium development that hinted at having once been a warehouse. Floyd lived in unit five. He answered my second ring smoking a pipe, wearing Top-Siders and white duck pants and a short-sleeved khaki safari jacket. His hair was blond and longish and his mustache was thick and shagged over his upper lip. He was flawlessly tanned and was probably thought a hunk by sexually liberated young women.

I said, "Art Floyd?"

He smiled. "Absolutely," he said.

"My name is Spenser, and I want to talk with you about a kid named Ginger Buckey."

Floyd squinted at me, his bright blue eyes narrowing effectively. "Gee," he said, "I'm sorry, but I don't think I know anyone by that name."

"Oh, darn," I said. "I was so hoping you would. How about Perry Lehman?"

Floyd held the squint, his cheeks dimpling engagingly as he smiled in honest puzzlement.

"Gee, mister," he said, "are you sure you've got the right guy? I don't know any of these people."

I put the flat of my hand against his chest and pushed him back into his living room and closed the front door behind us.

"Take your goddamned hands off me," Floyd said.

"Hand," I said. "It was only one hand."

Floyd was tall and slender and soft. He looked hard at me for a moment and then dropped his eyes.

"You're going to get yourself in real serious trouble," Floyd said.

"I'm used to it," I said. The living room was sunken and the dining room was two stairs up. I went and sat on the edge of the dining level. "You are a pimp, Arthur. A while ago you went up to Portland, Maine, and bought a young woman named Ginger Buckey from a whorehouse called Magic Massage. I want to know what you did with her."

Habit is hard to break. Floyd gave me his upward-mobile smile again. "Well, damn," he said. "I just don't know what to tell you."

I sat on the edge of the dining room and rested my weight on my hands and didn't say anything.

Floyd glanced at the front door. Somewhere in the house there was music playing: the Beatles' "Penny Lane." Floyd glanced at the phone behind me, through the dining room, in the kitchen. He looked back at me.

"Listen, guy," he said. "Let's get this straight before you get in so deep over your head that you can't get out. I can push some buttons and pull some switches on you that'll make your head spin."

"Excessive," I said. "Buttons, or switches. Either one would have been enough."

"I'm not joking," Floyd said. He frowned seriously. "I know some people who will swat you like a fly."

"Name one," I said.

Floyd opened his mouth and closed it.

I smiled. "If you threaten me with your big connections you'll be answering my question."

"You'll find out," he said.

"Yes," I said, "I will."

The Beatles were now singing "Maxwell's Silver Hammer." It was okay but it wasn't the Ink Spots. Floyd looked at the door again. Then back at me. He put his hands in his side pockets. His pants were the kind that didn't have back pockets. Don't want to ruin the bun line.

"One phone call and I can have you killed," Floyd said.

"If the people you call feel like doing it," I said, "or can."

Beyond Floyd's front window, behind a gray rustic fence, the boatyard was busy. An apparatus like a mobile dry dock was being used to shuttle yachts to the water. Everything moved very slowly but without surcease.

Floyd moved away from me slightly, toward the door. I got up and went past him to the door and leaned against it. He looked at me. I looked at him. The Beatles moved into "Hey Jude." They weren't the Mills Brothers either.

"What do you want?" Floyd said.

"I want to know what you did with Ginger Buckey after you brought her back from Portland."

"Why do you care?"

I didn't answer.

"I don't know anything about you," Floyd said. "You push in here, ask me a bunch of questions, block my way when I try to leave. I don't know anything about you. Why don't you get out of here."

I smiled at him. He walked across the room and sat on the edge of the dining level, as I had, then he stood up and walked back and leaned against the wall opposite me. He tilted his head to the side a bit and stared at me. The Beatles were still singing "Hey Jude."

"Okay," Floyd said. "You want to know what happened to her when I brought her down."

I nodded.

"I got her a job," Floyd said. "Good job at the Crown Prince Club."

"Hostess," I said.

"Sure. Chance to meet some class people and make some real money."

"And share it with you," I said.

Floyd shook his head. "No. Absolutely not. I took a finder's fee on this. I don't live off the earnings."

"The minute I saw you I knew you had the right stuff," I said.

"Well, I don't live off the earnings," he said. He looked a little sulky.

"We're proud of you back home, Artie."

"You want anything else?" he said.

"Nope."

"Then why don't you just leave," he said.

"It's just that I was breathless with admiration there for a minute," I said. "Hard to tear myself away."

"Try," he said.

The Beatles were singing "Michelle." They weren't the Platters either. Or the Ravens. Too bad.

"A thing is what it is," I said to Floyd, "and not something else."

He looked blank and pointed to the door and I departed.

19

It was Memorial Day and Susan and I packed a picnic and went canoeing on the Concord River. Actually I went canoeing and Susan went riding in the front of the canoe in a one-piece bathing suit catching some rays and occasionally trailing the fingers of her left hand in the water. The river was quiet and flat and gentle. Trees arched over it often and made the surface of the water dapple with shade. There were others on the river, as there usually were, but it was not crowded.

"We'll head upstream going out," I said. "So it'll be downstream coming back and we're tired."

"I don't expect to be tired," Susan said. She was facing me, her eyes closed, her face turned toward pre-summer sunshine. Her paddle lay on the floor of the canoe beside the red-and-white Igloo cooler.

"Must be all that Nautilus training," I said.

She smiled without opening her eyes.

It was easy paddling, the current was very gentle and I wasn't hurrying to get anywhere. Some kids were fishing from the shore. One of them spoke to Susan.

"Hey, lady," he said. "There's snapping turtles in here must weigh fifty pounds. I wouldn't put my hands in the water like that."

Susan kept her eyes closed but she pulled her hand back.

"Egad," she said.

"Nature red in tooth and claw," I said.

"Confirms your view of the world, I suppose," Susan said.

"I suppose."

"A lovely world with danger just beneath."

"Doesn't make the world less lovely," I said.

"Maybe makes it more," Susan said.

"Death is the mother of beauty?"

She opened her wonderful large eyes and looked at me and said, "Maybe." Her look was always kinetic. It always had the weight of mischief and passion and intelligence in it.

"How about prostitution," I said. "Got any thoughts on that?"

"Probably hard to generalize," Susan said, "though it's a pretty good bet that most prostitutes are working from a pathological base."

The backyards of many houses came down to the river in the section past the Concord Bridge, and the smell of barbecued hamburger drifted past us.

"But not necessarily the same pathological base," I said.

Susan nodded. Her bathing suit was cut fashionably high at the side and her thighs looked strong and smooth.

"A pathological base being another way to say that they're whacko."

She smiled. "That's the technical term for it. But it's a little broad, no pun intended, I would think, and my experience tells me that people choose to be whores for reasons which, when discovered, I would attempt to treat therapeutically."

"Aside from needing money," I said.

"Aside from that. Many people need money, not all of them choose to be prostitutes in order to earn it."

"How about they enjoy sex?" I said. The sun was warm on my back as I paddled slowly, letting the canoe slide along gently between strokes, listening to Susan. I had a pleasant sweat developing.

"Again it's hard to generalize, but I would guess that prostitution has little to do with sex."

"Patricia Utley says that the men and women involved in the transaction tend not to like one another."

The sun, as it got higher, reached more of the river and the dappling of shade contrasted more sharply.

"Sexual activity, unredeemed by love, or at least passion, is not the most dignified of activities," Susan said. "It offers good opportunities for degradation."

"For both parties," I said.

"For both parties.

"On the other hand," Susan said, "finding a way to satisfy pathological needs does not always make life untenable. Failing to satisfy the need makes it untenable. Many whores may be in a state of equilibrium."

"Meaning maybe they're better off being whores?"

"Sure, put that way, it's the decision we reached on April Kyle three years ago."

"But," I said.

"But," Susan said, "finding a way to fulfill a pathological need is not as satisfactory an answer as treating the need."

"But April wouldn't."

"Not then," Susan said. "Maybe not ever. Depends on how much pressure she feels."

"Tough way to look at it," I said.

"Psychology is a tough-minded business," Susan said. "As tough as yours. Maybe tougher. There's not much room for romanticism."

"Noted," I said.

"Do you know where April is?"

"Not yet, but I have hold of one end."

Susan smiled at the metaphor. "I'll bet you do," she said. "And when you find her?"

"We'll see. Depends on her situation," I said. "Let's eat."

We slid around a gentle meander in the river into a cove with a small strip of sand along the water's edge. I beached the canoe on the sand and Susan held it while I climbed out with the Igloo cooler.

We sat against the low banking together while I opened a bottle of white zinfandel. We each had a plastic glass of it and ate a smoked-turkey sandwich on whole wheat. Our shoulders touched. There was no one on this stretch of the river.

"Do you think a natural setting enhances lovemaking?" I said.

Susan sipped a little of her wine. She ate a small wedge of Crenshaw melon. She gazed up at the sky, and pursed her lips. She looked at the slate-colored river.

"No," she said, "I don't think so."

"Oh," I said. I swallowed a bit of smoked salmon on pumpernickel.

"But it doesn't do it any harm either," she said, and leaned her head into the place where my neck joins my shoulders. I kissed her on top of her head. She put her wine down and put her arms around me and kissed me on the mouth. I could taste the wine and melon. I could feel the rush I always felt.

Getting her out of the bathing suit was a bitch.

But worth it.

20

The Crown Prince Club was located at the end of an alley off Boylston Street near the Colonial Theatre. There was a heavy dark oaken door with a brass crown canted at a rakish angle just above the peephole. An antique brass turnbell handle projected from the middle of the door. I turned it and a bell rang distantly inside. Beside the door was a slot for card keys so that the members could go right in without ringing. It was three-thirty in the afternoon and no members were in sight.

The door opened. The guy who opened it was at least six four and looked like a nineteenth-century British soldier in the King's African Rifle Brigade. He had on a red tunic and a white pith helmet and gold epaulets, and his round black face was shiny and severe.

He said, "Yes, sir?"

I said, "I'm thinking of joining the club. Is there anyone I can talk to?"

"I'm sorry, sir, club memberships are not presently available."

"Damn," I said. "Tony Marcus told me that there was an opening."

The doorman looked at me instead of through me. "Mr. Marcus?"

"Yes, Tony sent me over. Said he'd talked with Perry Lehman about it."

"Mr. Lehman?"

"Yeah, said Perry could fix me up. I'm new in town."

"If you'd step in, sir, I'll ask our marketing director to speak with you."

"Thanks."

I went into the foyer. It was paneled in the same kind of dark oak that the front door was made of, and lit by Tiffany lamps. On the right wall was a high, narrow fireplace, and above it a painting of a horse that might have been by George Stubbs. The doorman gestured me to a large red leather chair near the fireplace. On a table beside the chair was a sandalwood box of cigars and a decanter of port, and several squat thick glasses.

"Please help yourself, sir," he said, "while I speak with Miss Coolidge."

I sat and the doorman disappeared through a door on the opposite side of the room. I poured myself a glass of port. The heft of the glass in my hand was masculine and weighty. There were two other paintings on the walls. One opposite the entrance door was of a black-and-white English spaniel curled up beside several recently shot partridge. The other, beside the door through which the

Royal Zulu had departed, was of a British officer mounted on a red roan horse looking directly at me. A vaguely desert background rolled away behind him. The sun never sets on the British Empire.

I had drunk about half the wine when a brisk middle-aged woman appeared in the doorway with the big black man. She strode into the room.

"I'm Gretchen Coolidge," she said. "Would you come with me, please."

"Sure."

The doorman stepped aside and I followed Gretchen Coolidge out of the waiting room and down a short corridor to an elevator. She gestured me in and we went up five floors and stopped and the doors slid silently open onto a brilliantly sunlit glass-canopied space. Compared with the dark Edwardian elegance of the waiting room the brilliance of the fifth floor was overpowering.

I followed Gretchen out into a corridor of potted plants to a large circular pool in the center of the room. The plants were exotic flowering types that I didn't recognize, but the scent of them and the density of colors was intense. Beside the pool a man sat at an emerald cube of a desk in a silk bathrobe talking into a silver telephone.

Gretchen Coolidge said, "Please sit down."

I sat near the desk in an angular chrome chair with green upholstery. Gretchen sat next to me. The guy at the desk continued to listen to the phone, nodding slightly. I looked around.

Gretchen Coolidge looked to be in her early forties. She had prominent cheekbones and short blond hair and large black-rimmed aviator glasses. She wore a double-breasted gray suit with a fine pinstripe in it and a lavender shirt with a narrow lavender-and-gray dotted necktie. A lavender handkerchief showed in her breast pocket. Her hose were a paler shade of lavender with very pale gray patterns in them. And she wore sling-strap three-inch heels of a deeper lavender. Her nails were short and painted pink. Her lipstick was pink. Her teeth were very white and even. Her breasts were large and looked as if, freed from restraint, they'd be even larger. She had slim hips and her ankles were small.

The guy on the phone was Perry Lehman. I'd seen his picture enough to recognize him. He was smallish and had long black hair. He wore a thick gold chain around his neck with a diamond-studded miniature crown suspended from it. The crown was hung to the same rakish cant as the trademark on the front door. He was darkly tanned. His small hands were manicured. He smoked a large cigar as he listened on the phone. Taking it from his mouth occasionally to study it, admire the pale greenish precision of the wrapper.

He had a big diamond ring on the little finger of his

right hand. Where the silk robe gaped, there was a sprinkle of gray hair on his cocoa-butter chest.

He said into the phone, "Okay, bottom line is one million, no more. You crunch the figures any way you want to, but it's one million, no more."

He listened again, then nodded once and said "Yes," and hung up the phone. He let the chair tilt forward and touched a button on his desk phone. Actually *desk phone* didn't quite cover it. There were enough buttons and lights and switches to qualify it as a communications console. He leaned back again in his high-backed green leather swivel and put his feet up on the desk. He was barefooted. A black man even larger than the one downstairs came in from behind some greenery carrying a silver tray with a silver ice bucket with an open bottle of champagne in it. There was a tall fluted champagne glass on the tray. The black man placed the tray on a small glass table beside the desk and stepped back. He was wearing a regimental tunic with brass buttons and gold epaulets, like the guy downstairs. But this tunic was white. He was hatless, his hair cropped close to his head. He looked at me without expression.

Lehman said, "That will be fine, Brutus. I'll call if I need you." The black man nodded, about-faced, and marched out. Lehman took the champagne from the ice bucket and poured some into his glass, carefully, a little at a time, letting the bubbles settle. The champagne was Taittinger Blanc de Blancs. When he had filled his glass he took a mouthful, and closed his eyes and tipped his head back and let the wine trickle down his throat. When he had swallowed he opened his eyes and looked at me and said, "Ah, nectar of the gods."

"Actually that's a tautology," I said.

"Excuse me?" Lehman said.

"Nectar *is* the drink of the gods, no need to say nectar of the gods. It's like saying ambrosia of the gods. Better simply to say, 'Ah, nectar.' "

Lehman looked at Gretchen Coolidge.

"This gentleman says he is from Tony Marcus," she said. "He told Virgil that Mr. Marcus told him you would, ah, *fix him up.*"

"You an English teacher, pal?" Lehman drank more champagne.

"Pal," I said. "I always love guys that call me pal."

Out of the corner of my eye I saw the regimental beastie reappear near one of the palm trees, by the far edge of the pool.

Lehman stared at me.

Gretchen said, "Mr. Lehman is very busy, perhaps you could tell us exactly what you had in mind?"

"And why you think a recommendation from Tony

Marcus means a piss hole in the snow to me?" Lehman said.

"Ah, the lilt of your imagery, Perry."

Lehman flicked a glance at the big black man.

"If Gunga Din assaults me, Perry, you'll never find out what I want and the place will get all messy."

He glanced at the Rolex watch on his left wrist.

"You got one minute from now," he said, "to tell me what you want." He drank the rest of the champagne, pulled the bottle from the bucket and carefully poured some more.

"I'm backtracking a kid named Ginger Buckey. Art Floyd picked her up at a massage parlor in Portland, Maine, and brought her down here and put her in your club. I want to know where she went from here."

"I don't know any Art Floyd, or Ginger whatever."

"And you, Ms. Coolidge?" I said.

"I'm afraid I can't help either."

I turned my head and looked at the black man. He stared at me without expression.

"Et tu, Brutus," I said.

"Any other questions?" Lehman said.

"You haven't run across a woman named April Kyle, have you?"

Lehman shook his head. Gretchen shook her head. Brutus simply gazed at me.

"I thought this was a palace of pleasure," I said. "I'm not having any fun here at all."

Lehman drank more of his champagne. "That's 'cause you're not asking for the right things, cowboy." He put the champagne glass down, picked up his cigar and puffed on it. I thought a duck might come down from the ceiling but nothing happened. "And because you're just talking, you follow my meaning? You're not giving me anything."

"What would you like?" I said.

Lehman shrugged and took the cigar out of his mouth and looked at the end of it and smiled.

"Hey," he said. "I'm easy. How about your name, for instance? How about your connection with Marcus? How 'bout why you want to know all this shit? Stuff like that." He had another swig of the champagne and put the cigar back in his mouth and puffed on it and shifted in his seat and folded his hands on his small belly. Behind him against the far wall there was a bright red and blue parrot in a big gold cage. The parrot was eating a sunflower seed.

I fished a business card out of my shirt pocket and held it out. Gretchen took it and put it on Lehman's desk. He didn't look at it.

"It's a nice card," I said. "New design. Crossed blackjacks."

Lehman didn't change expression.

"Name's Spenser," I said. "With an *s*. I'm a private

detective and I'm doing two things. I'm looking for a kid named April Kyle, and I'm investigating the murder, in New York, of a kid named Ginger Buckey. I think they're connected."

"And why come to me?" Lehman said. "And what's this Tony Marcus shit."

"I came to you because I know Ginger Buckey ended up working downstairs, and the Tony Marcus"—I looked at Gretchen—"ah, doo doo, is because I figured his clout would get me in."

"Marcus got no clout with me," Lehman said. "I got the clout."

"Sure," I said. "But here I am."

"And how do you know that Ginger Fuckey or whatever her name is ended up here?"

"Buckey," I said. I winked at Gretchen Coolidge. "I have my sources," I said.

Gretchen seemed frozen. She sat with her hands folded, her knees together, reading a spot about halfway between me and Lehman.

"I want to know," Lehman said.

"So here we are," I said. "I know something you want to know, and you know something I want to know."

"Maybe I'll just have Brutus shake it out of you," Lehman said.

"Maybe Brutus can't," I said.

I could hear Gretchen Coolidge breathing a little fast next to me. Lehman smoked his cigar and drank some champagne and smoked his cigar some more. There was a short furrow between his eyebrows. Probably trying to think. He looked at Brutus again. Immobile by the pool, still half shadowed by the palm fronds. He looked back at me.

"Okay," he said. "I can deal. Ginger Buckey worked for me for a while here and then later on at one of the other clubs, I don't remember which one, but Fetchin' Gretchen will be able to give you dates and places."

"I can check the files, Mr. Lehman," she said.

Lehman looked at me. "I keep telling Fetchin' she should get in the other end of the business." He nodded toward her hips. "She's sitting on a million bucks there."

Gretchen looked at her folded hands.

"You'd pay a few bucks for a ride on that, wouldn't you, Spence?"

"Even better than pal," I said, "I like guys that call me Spence. Especially pimps and guys that sell dirty pictures."

Lehman snorted. "Shit," he said, "aren't you a touchy bastard." He looked at his champagne glass. It was empty. He said, "Wanna pour me a little more, sweets."

Gretchen stopped looking at her hands and stood up and got the bottle and poured.

Lehman said, "I gave you what I had, let's hear yours."

"Art Floyd," I said.

"Sleazy little Ivy League prick," Lehman said.

Gretchen finished filling the glass and sat down. Lehman drank some.

"How'd you find Artie?" Lehman said.

"Usual way," I said. "I asked people, they told me."

"What's your connection with Marcus?"

"I know him, I talked with him. He doesn't like you."

Lehman laughed, "Tough shit for him."

"He said you were wired."

"He was right," Lehman said. "Connected, solid. Keep it in mind."

"Floyd told me he was connected too," I said.

Lehman laughed. "Yeah, he's connected all right. To me. I'm his fucking connection." He drank more champagne. He wasn't sipping anymore. "Connected." Lehman laughed again. "What a hot shit." He shook his head. He emptied the champagne glass and gestured at Gretchen. She poured out the rest of the bottle. Lehman saw the bottle was empty. He nodded at Brutus.

"We got anything else to talk about?" he said.

"Not this minute," I said. "But maybe we could get together again soon. I'd like to get your philosophy on things."

Lehman's face had a slight flush beneath the deep tan.

"If it's for sale buy it," he said. "If it's female fuck it. That's my philosophy, pal."

"Perhaps I should take Mr. Spenser to my office," Gretchen said, "and help him find out where Miss Buckey went."

Brutus appeared with a new bottle of champagne and put it in the ice bucket.

"Pour me a little more nectar, Miss Efficient Sufficient," Lehman said. "Then you can go."

Gretchen poured his champagne. I stood.

"Remember," Lehman said. "Buy it or fuck it—sometimes both."

"Words to live by," I said. And followed Gretchen out.

21

Gretchen's office was two floors down. Mauve walls, pale mint moldings, a gray lacquered desk with a mauve wash, purple silk flowers in a chrome vase on the desk. There was a computer on a black worktable coupled to a word processor. Against one wall were two black file cabinets. The window was covered in chrome-colored Levolor blinds, the kind with the narrow slats. A low marble table stood in front of the window. On it was a chrome water carafe and two violet-colored water glasses. There was a gray-and-black striped couch opposite her desk.

"Please sit down, Mr. Spenser, while I see what I have on Ginger Buckey."

I sat. "Must be a real treat," I said, "working for Perry Lehman."

"This is a very challenging opportunity," she said.

"Um," I said.

"The marketing schemata is one of the most energetic conceptualizations I've ever implemented."

She was thumbing through folders in the second drawer of one of the file cabinets.

"Um."

She paused. And turned toward me. "Mr. Spenser, I have an MBA from the Wharton School. The women in my graduating class are averaging thirteen thousand a year less than the men." She glanced at the label on one file folder and put it back. "I'm earning eight thousand more than the men."

"Liberation," I said.

"Whatever Mr. Lehman's attitudes are, he pays me what I'm worth. It's a kind of liberation that translates directly."

"What exactly is the conceptual schemata of this operation other than smut peddling, so to speak?"

Gretchen turned holding a folder in her right hand and looked at me. "You're incredible," she said. "That's like saying what's the marketing strategy for Coca-Cola other than selling soft drinks."

She closed the file drawer and stepped to her desk and sat down. She put the folder on the desk before her and straightened it carefully so all four corners aligned with the four corners of her blotter.

"There's a classic phrase in marketing," she said. She put both elbows on her desk and placed her hands together as if she were praying and rested her chin on the tips of her fingers. "Sell the sizzle, not the steak."

"Classic," I said.

"We're not, as you put it, peddling smut. We're selling self-image. We're selling realized fantasy. We are marketing fully realized life-style—masculine, sexually fulfilled, powerful, solid, complete, energized by a sense of the permanent in clothing and wines, in dining and entertainment. We're saying simply every man is a crown prince."

"And you're making eight thousand a year more than your male classmates."

"And implementing the whole concept," she said. "It's not just the money, Spenser." She dropped her hands onto the desk and leaned forward. "I'm in charge."

"Until Perry tells you to get undressed and you say no."

She shook her head. "He talks a little rough, but there's nothing like that." She shook her head again. "Nothing. I find it offensive that you'd suggest it."

"At least I assumed you'd say no," I said.

"And if I said yes?"

"I'd figure you had a cast-iron stomach," I said.

"I have no relationship with Mr. Lehman beyond a business relationship." She opened the file folder and studied it. She frowned slightly.

"Ginger Buckey came to us in August last year. She remained here as a hostess until this May, when she resigned."

"To do what?" I said.

Gretchen shook her head. "I don't know. The girls come and go. There was nothing outstanding about Ginger. There's no reason we should remember her, and quite frankly I don't."

"Lehman did," I said.

"Mr. Lehman has a remarkable memory."

"May I see the file?"

"No, I'm sorry, but it is confidential. All our files are." I thought about taking it. She must have sensed that because she got up briskly and put it back in the file and locked it.

"Perhaps you'd like to see some of the facilities here?" she said, and opened her office door. Another of the King's African Rifles was standing at parade rest.

"Place looks like the Grambling locker room," I said.

Gretchen smiled and we went along the corridor past the sentry and into the elevator.

"First floor is health club and screening," she said.

"Nicely done," I said.

"I beg your pardon?"

"You were afraid I might snatch the file on you so you locked it up and walked me out into the corridor past the footman without even hinting at distress. Very smooth."

"I had no such fear," Gretchen said.

"You should have," I said. "The minute you said it was confidential I wanted to see it."

"There's nothing in that file, Mr. Spenser. Confidentiality is simply our policy."

"Sure," I said.

We got off the elevator and walked a short paneled corridor and into the health club. It was carpeted and mirrored and staffed with female training assistants in white short shorts and yellow halter tops. To the left a waterfall cascaded down a marble wall into a full-size Olympic pool. There were two men in Speedo racing suits swimming laps. To the right was a bar that sold beer, wine coolers, Perrier, yogurt shakes, and fruit juice. There were also health sandwiches listed on a blackboard. Today's special was jack cheese, avocado slices, sunflower seeds, and alfalfa sprouts on seven-grain bread. The rest of the room was devoted to Nautilus equipment, a profusion of it in chrome and colors. Several men in state-of-the-art sweats were working out, while a training assistant stood by with their chart, offering water after each exercise and cheering them on.

"We have the most complete Nautilus setup in Massachusetts," Gretchen said. "We also have massage rooms, whirlpool, steam, sauna, inhalant and tanning rooms, each staffed by a highly trained professional."

I opened a door marked MASSAGE. There was a plump guy getting a massage, a towel draped across his butt. The masseuse was dressed like the training assistant except that she had on yellow high-heeled backless shoes.

We moved on and looked at the racquetball courts. We went into the screening room, a small movie theater, attended by a young woman dressed like an old-time movie usher.

"We run a continuous program of adult entertainment," Gretchen said, "rather like the old newsreel theaters in train stations."

The current feature showed a woman wearing horn-rimmed glasses and white stockings having intercourse with a skinny black-haired guy on the banister of a flight of stairs.

"Precarious," I said.

"We have a library of several thousand adult film classics," Gretchen said.

The woman on the screen told her lover in an excited way that she wanted "more, more, more."

"Classics," I said.

We went back in the elevator and went up a flight.

"This is the lounge and library," Gretchen said.

It was a big room lined on three walls with books. Along the fourth wall was a bar. There were leather chairs and reading lamps and a cocktail waitress dressed like Hollywood's idea of a prim librarian stood near the bar with her round tray. No one else was there. The titles were mostly simple pornography with a scattering of works like *The Decameron*, to make the readers feel less like perverts. We moved on.

There was a restaurant staffed with waitresses dressed like French maids, a nightclub that opened after nine. I didn't ask what the waitresses wore.

"What's on the fourth floor?" I said.

"Guest rooms for the members."

"Complete with hostesses?" I said.

Gretchen smiled. "All of our girls are hostesses," she said.

"Which kind of hostess was Ginger Buckey?" I said.

"I'm not sure, I think she was assigned to the guest floor."

"What are the duties of a guest floor hostess?" I said.

"Maid service, butlery. There's a pantry there, they are a bit like a concierge, and there are enough so that the members get immediate personal attention at any hour."

"Turn-down service, two chocolate mints on the pillow, that sort of thing," I said.

"Among many others," Gretchen said. "The girls are there to serve the needs of the members."

"Including sexual service," I said.

"We are not a house of prostitution, Mr. Spenser. Nor are we a college dormitory. The girls are free to form relationships with the guests, should they choose to."

"And if they don't choose to?"

"Our policy is very simple and it's part of our success: The member is always right. If there's a complaint about a girl, she is disciplined."

"What kind of discipline?"

"It depends on the complaint, fines, dismissal, other things."

"What other things?"

"I'm sorry again, Mr. Spenser. Specific company policy is confidential. I'm sure you understand."

"Any complaints about Ginger Buckey?"

"None," Gretchen said.

"How nice," I said. She seemed to remember Ginger after all.

We were back on the first floor, in the Edwardian foyer.

"So what do you think of our operation," Gretchen said.

"I think that if Walt Disney had been obsessed with sex and dominance, and was uncertain of his manhood and had grown up reading the novels of H. Rider Haggard and had the sensibility of a dung beetle he'd have founded a chain of clubs just like this."

The bones in Gretchen's face seemed more prominent. "I see," she said. "Have you any further questions?"

"No," I said. "I'm going home and take a shower."

22

It was Tuesday and an unassertive spring rain was coming straight down. I had picked up two corn muffins and an extra large coffee, black, no sugar, at the Dunkin' Donuts shop near the corner of Exeter Street and walked down Boylston to my office on the corner of Berkeley. I had eaten the muffins at my desk and I was standing at my office window looking down at the street and drinking the rest of the coffee when the door opened. I turned. In came Brutus.

He was out of uniform. His massive upper body straining inside a silver Porsche racing jacket. He had on designer jeans and Reebok track shoes.

I said, "Tell me your name isn't really Brutus."

"Jackson," he said, "Charles Jackson."

"Where'd you play ball?" I said.

"Morgan State."

"Step slow for the pros?" I said.

Jackson grinned. "Step and a half," he said.

"You enjoy being called Brutus by a twerp like Perry Lehman?"

Jackson grinned more. "Shit," he said, "don't make no difference to me. Kind of money he pays me he can call me motherfucker, he wants."

He took my card from the side pocket of his silver jacket. The jacket was half unzipped and I could see that he was shirtless. I didn't see any sign of a gun though he could have had an ankle holster.

"Picked this up off Perry's desk when he went for his nap," Jackson said. "He usually take one, 'bout two bottles a champagne."

I nodded toward a chair. Jackson looked at it carefully, decided he'd fit, and sat gently. He stretched his legs out in front of him and crossed his ankles.

"Tell me 'bout Ginger," he said.

"She was hooking in New York. Not very good. Street hooking around Times Square. I met her and talked with her. Couple days later she got shot to death. Nobody knows who shot her."

Jackson nodded.

"She had a pimp named Robert Rambeaux, I talked with him. Couple of days later he got beat up and is now scared to death."

"So if she's dead, how come you're looking for her?"

"I'm looking for a kid named April Kyle," I said. "She disappeared the same time Ginger got killed and Rambeaux got beat up. I haven't got a lead on her. I had a lead on Ginger. So I'm following Ginger, see if April turns up along the way. There's a connection, and eventually I'll find it."

"She was from Maine," Jackson said.

"Yeah, I know, I went up there, talked with her father."

Jackson nodded. "She was a good kid," he said. "Not smart as hell; but a lot of us ain't. Had a hard life. Artie Floyd brought her in couple of years ago, bought her from a place in Maine."

"I know," I said. "Finder's fee, he called it. Father sold her to the Maine place in the first place."

"Like I say, had a hard life. Broke her down pretty much, didn't have too much sass left by the time she come to the club. But they clean her up and dress her nice and she makes good money and nice tips fucking the members up on the fourth floor."

"That's how it's done?" I said. "Tips?"

"Pretty much. Broads get minimum wage for being hostesses, members tip them for fucking."

"The club get a cut?"

Jackson shook his head. "Don't need it. Make the dough on memberships and booze, and the magazine and the resorts and shit. The poontang just a fringe benefit, make the asshole members feel good."

"So where'd Ginger go?"

"She went to the islands with a member, never came back."

"Which islands?"

"St. Thomas, got a club resort there."

"What's the member's name?" I said.

Jackson shook his head. "Don't know. Never know. Just noticed one day she gone and later got a card from St. Thomas. Guess she didn't stay with him."

"Guess not," I said. "When she go?"

" 'Bout Christmas."

"You got the card?" I said.

"Shit, man, you think I keep postcards? I read it and threw it away. How 'bout Miss Coolidge, she tell you anything?"

"Just that Ginger worked there and then left. Dates are right."

"They ain't going to tell you shit," he said. "Something funny 'bout it all."

"What?" I said.

Jackson shrugged, "Don't know. Just, everybody don't talk about Ginger, or where she gone."

"You ever ask?"

"Naw, I just go 'bout my business there, do my Brutus act, make sure the members don't get out of hand, make sure the girls behave, make sure old Marse Lehman got champagne. I start asking questions and they fire my ass and I have to go to work. I hate work."

"Never much liked it myself," I said. "Wouldn't they fire your ass for talking to me?"

"Sure, I just figure you won't tell them."

"Do other girls go off with members?"

Jackson put one of his big Reeboks on the edge of my desk.

"Some," he said. "Not too often."

"How does it come about?" I said.

"Come about," Jackson said, "shit. You talk pretty fancy for a guy with a neck like mine."

"Sound mind in a healthy body," I said. "How does the going off with a member work?"

"Got me," Jackson said. "You understand I'm mostly window dressing. Big black dude stand around and look bad. Part of the look, you know? They actually go round to black schools and recruit ballplayers. Make old Perry feel bold have a few black studs standing by."

"Yowzah," I said.

Jackson shrugged. "You think you gonna play ball all your life, then you twenty-four and you finished and ain't no real market for running over offensive tackles. Better than stealing."

"And Perry's fun to be around."

Jackson shook his head. "Man's a douche bag," he said, "but he got a touch for money."

"When things are going bad," I said, "you can feel good about not being Perry Lehman."

"Cheer you right up, man," Jackson said.

"You know anything about how heavily he's connected?"

Jackson shook his head. "Nope. He talk like he got the heaviest connections you can get. But the man's a blowhard. He talk like that anyway, whether he got connections or no."

I nodded. "True," I said. "Anything else I should know?"

"A lot you should know, man, but that's all I got to tell you."

I stood up. "Thank you," I said. "If there's something I can do for you sometime, I will."

Jackson stood up. We shook hands.

"Going down to the islands?" he said.

"Probably," I said.

"Enjoy," he said, and turned and left the room.

I called Patricia Utley and made a proposal.

"I'm looking for April again," I said. "And I need a client."

"Running short of funds?" she said.

"Very," I said.

"I'm not in a charitable business," she said.

"I'm trying not to be either," I said. "We both have some interest in this kid."

"She's missing?"

"Un huh. And the kid I talked to, Ginger Buckey, is dead and Robert Rambeaux, the pimp, is bruised and scared, and something's going on, and nobody is telling me what."

"Did you go up to Maine?"

"Un huh."

"Is Vern Buckey the toughest man in Lindell?"

"Nope."

"You want me to hire you some more to find April?"

"Yes. You and I both have a . . . we know her. Most people don't. We invested some energy in her. Most people haven't."

"Good money after bad," Patricia Utley said.

"Yep."

"Okay," she said. "Do you need an advance?"

"Yes."

"I'll send it. Do you have any, ah, clues?"

"Not much," I said. "All I can think of is that Ginger and April are connected and maybe if I find out what happened with Ginger I'll be able to find what happened to April."

"What progress have you on Ginger?"

I told her.

"Perry Lehman?" she said.

"Yes."

"Crown Prince?"

"Yep. Know him?"

"Not personally, but anybody in the sex business knows his operation. Very impressive."

"He's a slime ball," I said.

"Oh, no doubt," she said. "I have heard stories. He pays well but he tends to use up a lot of girls, and I understand he has ties to the mob."

"So I hear."

"Very impressive operation, though," Patricia Utley said.

"That's what his marketing director told me. She says he's selling self-image."

"He's selling what I'm selling. He's just packaging it for national consumption."

"I prefer the cottage industry approach," I said. "Actually, if the truth be known, I prefer amateurism in this area."

"Tastes vary," she said. "Are you off to the Caribbean?"

"Yeah," I said. "It's tough, dirty work, but someone's got to go down there and do it."

"I knew you wouldn't flinch," she said. "How are you

going to go about it? If there is something amiss they'll not welcome you at the Crown Prince Club."

"I thought I'd acquire a membership under false pretenses," I said.

"Well, I trust your resourcefulness," she said. "I'll send you your money."

"Thank you."

"You're welcome."

I hung up and sat back at my desk and put my feet up and tried to think of someone I knew who was sleaze berry enough to join the Crown Prince Club. And kind enough to lend me his membership.

23

I couldn't find anyone I knew who had the right combination of sleaze and kindness to get me into the St. Thomas Crown Prince, so I decided to wing it.

Susan and I flew on Pan Am via New York and got into St. Thomas early in the afternoon. The corrugated-iron air terminal on the island looked like an exhibition hall at the Minnesota State Fair, full of odd little booths.

We picked up a rental car and a map and drove the narrow road through Charlotte Amalie to Frenchman's Reef. The island looked as it ought to, a lot of greenery, a lot of flowers, cruise ships in the harbor, stuccoed tropical-looking buildings with red tile roofs rising along the island's central ridge. Frenchman's Reef was a big Holiday Inn with a good beach and ocean views and a balcony on each room big enough to dance on if you were a hamster.

In our room Susan said, "What first? A swim or a margarita?"

"I'm here to work," I said.

"But I'm not," Susan said. "I'm here as a paid companion."

"Paid," I said. "I hadn't heard about paid. What is it going to cost me?"

"A frozen margarita whenever I want it," she said.

"Okay, but for that you have to come across."

Susan put her hands on either side of my face and kissed me on the mouth lightly.

"You jerk," she said, "you could have gotten it free." She spoke with her lips brushing mine.

"I never had a head for business," I said.

"Speaking of head," she said, and then started to giggle.

"Dr. Silverman," I said, holding her away from me at arm's length with my hands on her shoulders. "You are a highly educated Jewish psychotherapist approaching middle years. And here, in this sophisticated island hideaway, I find you talking dirty and giggling like an oversexed teenage shiksa."

"Talk to me, baby," Susan murmured, "whisper in my ear."

And we both began to laugh and I pulled her back in against me.

An hour and twenty minutes later we went down to the beach in our bathing suits and sat at the outdoor bar.

"You owe me five margaritas," Susan said.

"Cheap at ten," I said. We ordered two. Frozen for Susan, on the rocks for me. Frozen went in too slowly.

"People are looking at you," Susan said.

"My massive upper body?" I said. "My wasp waist? My Romanesque profile outlined against the azure sea?"

"The several bullet scars against the pale white skin? Don't you ever work on a tan?"

"My face and neck are tan," I said.

"And your forearms. The rest of you looks like Casper the burly ghost."

"We northern Europeans don't care to be made sport of by a swarthy Levantine."

"Well, you need to be careful," she said, "or you will burn badly."

"I'm too tough," I said.

"I'd smite the sun if it offended me," Susan murmured.

I grinned and held out my hand toward her and she took it and we sat in our beach chairs and looked at the water holding hands. My margarita had disappeared. Susan's glass was still half full. I gestured at the woman tending bar. She made me another one and brought it over and took my empty glass.

"Have you a plan?" Susan said.

"I've been executing it," I said, "for the last hour and a half."

"Besides that."

"After dinner," I said, "I'm going to wander over to

the Crown Prince Club and see if I can mix and mingle and look like an upward mobile nitwit with severe sexual dysfunction."

"And blend in with the clientele."

"Yes," I said.

The sea was very blue and the sand in front of us was sugar-white and the waves came in steady but not aggressive. The beach was half full of people in brief bathing suits. The cellulite count was high.

"I assume my presence would be inappropriate."

I nodded and finished off my second margarita. "You have several disabilities," I said. "You are an adult, you appear intelligent, and there seems to be some force in you. I'm afraid that even if they didn't catch on that you weren't a hostess, you might scare all the customers. They're not used to intelligent adults. Probably give them the bends."

"You say I'm not a nymphet?"

"Afraid not."

Susan took a big gulp of her margarita. "Damn," she said, "you put your faith in aerobics and what does it get you."

"Hell," I said, "I'm not a nymphet either."

"That's true," she said. "It helps."

She finished the margarita and stood and walked into the water. I went after her, and for an hour we swam and rolled in the affable surf under the Caribbean sky near the bar.

Then we had another margarita and went back to the room and got ready for dinner. I've had tougher duty.

We went to dinner at Secret Harbor.

"I came here once when I was married," Susan said. "It was very nice."

The dining room was under a roof, but without walls, within feet of the water. The air was pleasant. The tables were well spaced. The waitress was a young woman from Quincy, Massachusetts. We began with a bottle of Iron Horse champagne and had duck with a lime and raspberry sauce and a salad of limestone lettuce and two slices of fruit tart. We had a second bottle of champagne with dinner and afterward we each had two Baileys on the rocks. It was nearly ten-thirty when we finished. We spoke hardly at all and looked at each other almost all the time. The ocean murmured very softly and somewhere people were dancing to swing music and the sound of it drifted in on the quiet air.

"I've revised my plan," I said.

"Really?"

"Yes. My plan now is to go back to the hotel with you and go to sleep and get up tomorrow, fresh as a sea trout, and go over to the Crown Prince Club and knock them dead."

"At eight in the morning?"

"Well, maybe we'll have breakfast and swim awhile and have lunch and swim awhile and I'll go at cocktail time."

"The man of steel is full and sleepy," Susan said.

"I think there was krypton in that drink," I said.

"You're kind of cute when you're human," she said.

"And when I'm not?"

She reached over and took my hand and there was no banter in her voice.

"You're lovely," she said.

24

The Crown Prince Club on the east end of the island looked like a sugar plantation designed by Ralph Lauren. There were cottages constructed from simulated coconut logs and thatched with simulated palm fronds scattered among real palm trees over a couple of acres of absolutely immaculate land. Near the long white beach was the Princedom, a long house built of the same materials as the cottages where the dining room, bar, and workout room were located. There was no fence but a number of strapping blackamoors in raspberry Lacoste shirts and white shorts strolled about the grounds, their biceps gleaming darkly in the dappling shade of the palm trees.

On the beach many of the women were topless, and both sexes were smeared with oil and glistening in a tan frenzy. Waitresses in minimal designer castaway outfits moved among the sunbathers with drinks on trays. Dimly through the palms I could see some tennis courts in use and in front of the Princedom a buffet was being set up next to a semipermanent bar emplacement of simulated palm logs. I moved toward the buffet, where people in white slacks and flowered shirts were already beginning to gather. In the center of the buffet table was a fountain of amber liquid. There were punch cups set out and people were filling them from the fountain. It looked like rum punch. There were large platters of oysters on the table, and lobster tails and cold meats. There was fruit salad in a scooped-out watermelon, and assorted bread and rolls. There was cheese and salad and nearby a whole pig turned slowly on an electric rotisserie. I looked closely. It wasn't Perry Lehman. I shrugged. I was used to disappointments.

Nobody said *hey you* to me. No one required me to show my membership card, nobody seemed to notice that I was somewhat old and somewhat large and somewhat well conditioned for the group assembled here at the Princedom. I had a cup of punch. I was right, it was rum. I glanced over the assorted buffet items. A man in a white chef's hat appeared carrying a huge bowl of jumbo shrimp and set the bowl down on the table.

"Local catch?" I asked.

"No, man, there don't be no local catch."

"You mean there's no fish around here? We're in the middle of the ocean."

"There's fish, man, there's no fisherman."

"Except maybe a fisher of tourists," I said.

"You got it, man." He went away back in a side door to the Princedom. I took a shrimp. On the long veranda of the Princedom a three-piece combo was getting organized. There was an electric keyboard, drums, and bass. Two more men in white coats appeared carrying a great tub of iced beer. They set it on an upturned barrel and went back into the Princedom.

A voice next to me said, "Hadn't you ought to try the oysters?"

It was an oriental woman, Chinese maybe, or part Chinese. She had long shiny black hair brushed back away from her face. She was wearing an aquamarine-colored bikini with a short white lace shirt over it. The collar was turned up and the loose sleeves were pushed halfway up her smooth arms. She wore strapless high-heeled shoes. Her nails were painted the same aquamarine as the bikini and her lipstick was a pink so pale as to be nearly white. She had small breasts and firm thighs. A vaccination mark on her thigh meant she was probably older than she looked.

"I think that's a myth," I said.

"Oysters?" She widened her eyes and glanced at me from a slightly oblique angle. Enticing.

"Yeah, I don't think they do anything for potency."

She smiled, still looking slightly sideways at me. "Oh, that's too bad. Do you need any help with your potency?"

"Not as long as I take my powdered rhino horn," I said.

Her seductive sideways look shifted a bit to the hint of puzzlement, but she caught it, got it back in place, and smiled knowingly.

"Well, I hope you keep taking it," she said. "What's your name?"

"Chris Marlowe," I said.

"I'm Suki," she said. "Can I make you up a plate from the buffet?"

"I think that might be out of step with current feminist attitudes," I said.

"Oh, pooh," Suki said. "Oriental women are trained to please men"—she smiled cutely—"in every way," she said. "It is our pleasure."

"Heavens," I said, "what would Eleanor Smeal say?"

Suki shook her head. "I don't know Eleanor, but I know you, Chris, and I want to give you whatever you want."

"I can dig it," I said. "Just make me up a light assortment. I'll take the grapes with the skins."

Suki looked confused again for a moment, but she smiled right on through it and went to get me a plate. I had a second rum punch while I was waiting. The band began to play. Their first selection was a slightly overarranged version of Ricky Nelson's song "Garden Party." There was a good crowd around now. A lot of the people at the buffet table were women making up plates for men.

Serving men was apparently not an exclusively oriental tradition.

Suki came back with my plate. She had quite carefully arranged a little of almost everything.

"Let's go to the veranda," she said, "and you can enjoy your meal."

"Sure," I said, and followed her as she carried the dinner plate ahead of me up onto the porch.

We sat together on a wicker love seat with a low table in front of us. The band had started to play "Sleepy Lagoon." Clearly they were working thematically. Suki offered me an oyster on a small fork. I ate it.

I said, "A bit more sauce on the next one, my dear."

"Certainly, kind master," she said, and smiled and put a little more cocktail sauce on the next oyster. "I'm sorry we don't have any powdered horn."

"It's okay," I said. "I'll make do with oysters."

"Oh, Chris," she said. "So, are you married?"

I winked at her. "Of course not," I said.

She smiled at me and put a shrimp in my mouth. "I believe you," she said. "Which bungalow you in?"

"Over there," I said. "Why do you ask?"

"Oh, I don't know," Suki said. "In case I needed you later on, or"—she looked up at me as she put a piece of Jarlsberg cheese on a cracker—"you needed me."

"You been working here long?" I said. Suki slid the

cracker and cheese between my lips as I asked her. I bit down on it and held it between my teeth and then lipped it in and chewed.

"I wouldn't call it work, Chris."

"Well, have you been playing here long?"

"Five years," Suki said. "Last May. Year-round. The weather is . . . well, you can't beat the weather."

"Sure can't," I said. "Is there wine?"

"Oh, Chris, I'm sorry," she said. "I'll get it. Red or white?"

"You choose, I want you to drink some too."

"Don't move," she said. "I'll be right back." She ran away toward the buffet table, smoothing her long black hair back from her forehead with both hands. All around me on the veranda were men being fed by women. Maybe the wine bottle would have a nipple on it. The trio began to play "In the Cool Cool Cool of the Evening."

Suki came back with a carafe of white wine and two glasses. She poured one for me and then herself. She handed me mine and raised her glass at me.

"To love," she said.

"And lust," I said. We clinked glasses and drank. Suki smiled at me, her eyes widened. "There's a difference?" she said.

"Not here," I said.

We both drank some wine. It was jug wine, served very cold.

"Ginger Buckey still around?" I said.

"You know Ginger?" Suki said.

"Sure," I said. "Who doesn't?"

"She never really worked here," Suki said. "She used to come down with Warren."

Suki had tucked her legs up under her on the love seat and was leaning against me, her head on my shoulder, looking up at my face as she talked. She drank her wine.

"I don't think she's been down since spring," she said.

I nodded and leaned forward and took a green grape from the plate and tucked it into her mouth.

"Now Chris is gonna feed Suki," she said. She had dropped her voice an octave and given it a slight purr. She took the grape in her mouth and sucked on it a little and rolled it around in her mouth. I think she was being seductive.

She chewed the grape and swallowed it.

"What else you gonna feed me, Chris?"

She had her wineglass in her left hand. I raised it, hand and all, to her lips and tilted it. She drank.

"She was working in Boston," I said, "when she came down with Warren?"

"Uh huh. She's a nice kid. Got to know her a little in training, you know? All us girls go through training together, one month a year, off to school. Mr. Lehman makes sure of everything."

"Really," I said.

"Can Suki have another grape, Chris?"

I slipped one in her mouth. She ate it sensuously. The old suck-the-grape come-on.

"That's how I know her," I said. "I'm from Boston, but I'm trying to place Warren—tall, slim black guy, light skin?"

Suki laughed. "God, no," she said. "Warren's white, about sixty, he's like a banker or something." She dropped her voice. "Very important." She laughed again. "Ginger said he was kind of kinky but I used to wonder if he could get it up."

"Oh, that guy, yeah, I think I've seen him around the club in Boston, what the hell is his name. Beatty? No, Burger?"

Suki said, "I never knew his last name."

"Wonder why they broke up," I said.

"I think they had a fight when they were down here. One day I noticed Warren went home without her."

"And she stayed?"

"No, she was gone too. I heard she took off with one of the musicians. Why? She know some tricks you think I don't know?"

"Naw, just asking. She was a good kid, and then I

hadn't seen her in a while. I thought she'd moved down here."

"This isn't a move, Chris. Down here is a promotion."

"Upward and onward," I said.

25

Suki and I danced a little on the broad veranda. It had verged into evening and the moon was out. On cue the band played "Blue Moon," "Moonglow," "Moonlight Becomes You," and were halfway into "Old Devil Moon" when Suki excused herself.

"Suki has to find the little girls' sandbox, Chris," she said.

"Hurry back," I said, cocking my head the way I was pretty sure Cary Grant did.

She disappeared into the Princedom. I had a thought. I walked over to the band and stood near them as they finished up "Old Devil Moon" with a big keyboard flourish.

"Before you guys break into "Moonlight Sonata," I said, "do you know Robert Rambeaux?"

"No, but hum a few bars and we'll fake it," the keyboard man said. He was a skinny black guy with a thin mustache. He liked his joke enough for a cool inward chuckle. The drummer did a soft rim shot.

"Everywhere I go," I said, "Henny Youngman. Didn't Rambeaux used to play down here?"

"Sure, man. Worked a lot of places on the island. Reed man."

"How come he left?"

"Woman trouble," the keyboard player said.

"Someone got pregnant?"

"Man, nobody gives a shit about that anymore," he said. "Got tied up with one of the hostesses, went off with her. Left the client with his dick in his hand, you know."

"That's old Robert," I said. "Always playing the wrong instrument. Was it Ginger?"

"That he run off with?" The keyboard player shrugged. "Got me, man, we gotta blow. Ain't time yet for a break."

I nodded. "What's next? 'How High the Moon'?"

The keyboard player grinned, nodded at the bassist, and launched into "Moon over Miami." I looked around. Suki was still busy in the little girls' sandbox. Seemed like a good time to boogie on out of the Crown Prince Club. So I did.

Driving back toward Frenchman's Reef I thought about Suki's feelings of rejection. Late in the evening without a client for the night. Probably too late to find another one, no tip tonight. She probably wouldn't have respected me in the morning anyway.

The roads on St. Thomas are narrow and they wind. The terrain is hilly and driving at night is slow. I got back to the hotel near midnight and went into the room. Susan was sitting up in bed reading *Common Ground* by J. Anthony Lukas.

I made a V sign at her with the first two fingers of my right hand.

"Being trained in people skills, I perceive that you feel triumphant," Susan said.

"I'll say. I was hand-fed my supper by an adoring Eurasian cutie," I said, "who then titillated me by suggestively eating a grape."

Susan put her book facedown, open, on her lap.

"Well," she said, "no wonder you feel triumphant."

"Also I found out that Ginger came down here with a banker-type sixtyish white guy from Boston and left him here and took off with Robert Rambeaux."

"Ah ha," Susan said.

"You remember my mention of Rambeaux?"

"The New York pimp."

"You do listen," I said.

"It's my training," she said.

"As a shrink?"

"No, as a woman," Susan said. "Hard to overcome early habits."

"Should we order up room service?" I said. "You could feed me something."

I sat on the bed beside her. She had on a lacy-topped copper-colored nightgown.

"I feed your ego nearly every day," she said. "That's enough." She took my hand. "How'd you find all this stuff out?"

"I asked," I said. "And of course the virile power of my masculine self was enough to entrance Suki. She'd have told me anything I asked."

"Suki?" Susan said.

"Un huh. And asking the band about Rambeaux was just sort of an inspiration."

"Unconscious integration," Susan said.

"That too," I said. "Besides, Suki told me that Ginger took off with one of the musicians."

"So now what," Susan said.

"We'll go to New York and discuss this further with Rambeaux."

"We will? When will we?" Susan said. She had moved my hand between her breasts and held it there.

"Well, not right away," I said. "Probably have to rest up a little first."

"Good thought," Susan said. "Perhaps you'd care to lie down on a comfortable psychologist?"

"Are you sure it will be restful?" I said.

"I hope not," she said.

"Need to figure out who Warren is," I said.

I had slid down on the bed beside her. I put my free arm around her. "I don't know if Warren fits, but he's a loose piece and I can't ignore him."

"Maybe you could ignore him for just a little while," Susan said.

"How little?" I said.

"It's up to you, big fella," Susan murmured.

"Then we'll ignore him for a large while," I said.

And we did.

26

We got back from St. Thomas on a Monday. Susan had patients on Tuesday, so I went to New York without her. Someone told me that the Parker Meridien had a health club, so this time I stayed there. Besides, it was but a few strides from the Russian Tea Room. It was my intention to keep going to the Russian Tea Room for lunch until someone recognized me. Or mistook me for someone. Or gave me a table downstairs.

To recover from the shuttle ride down, I went immediately to the health club in the hotel and did three sets of everything on the Nautilus machines. Then I rode one of the Exercycles for a half hour at a ten setting and limped back up to my room and took a shower. I bet I could bench press more than the maître d' at the Russian Tea Room. If he came to the health club, I wouldn't seat him either.

I went down into the high flossy lobby and had two bottles of Heineken beer in the lobby bar and felt sufficiently reinvigorated to try a walk uptown.

It was about four in the afternoon when I turned

down 77th Street from Fifth Avenue and about ten past four when I arrived in front of Robert Rambeaux's apartment. He didn't answer the bell. I rang some other bells but no one buzzed me in. I leaned against one wall of the entry and waited. At about four-forty a tall young man wearing a T-shirt that said JACOB'S PILLOW on it came out and I went in before the door closed behind him. He glanced at me as I went in and then moved on. The slow narrow elevator took me to Rambeaux's floor. I knocked on his door with no result. I wished I could open a door with a credit card like they did on TV, but all I ever did was screw up the card. I could kick it down.

I pressed my ear against the door to hear what was in there. If Robert was still scared and in there with a gun, kicking the door down would get me a faceful of .32 ammunition.

I didn't hear anything. But I smelled something. I knew what it was and I knew it had been a while if I smelled it through a closed door. I went back down in the elevator and out onto the street and found a pay phone. I dialed 911.

"I'd like to report a dead body," I said, "at 330 East 77th Street."

I met the patrol officers at the apartment and we went up with the super. I let them go in first. Old corpses aren't fun. The stench was strong when the super opened the door, and there was a buzz of flies.

The super left the key in the door and turned and went as fast as he could without running back down the stairs.

"Jesus Christ," one of the cops said, and pulled out a handkerchief and covered his mouth and nose and went in. His partner did the same and followed him in. I didn't.

An hour and a half later I was leaning on the front right fender of a patrol car, talking with Detective Second Grade Corsetti.

"No way to tell if it's Rambeaux," Corsetti was saying. "Have to wait for the ME to tell us."

"You didn't examine him closely?"

Corsetti wrinkled his nose. "Time I got here they'd hauled him off, I'm just telling you what the bodybaggers told me. You were, you get a close look?"

"I didn't want to be in the way," I said.

Corsetti nodded. "I know," he said. "I seen maybe eight, ten stiffs been dead like that, still can't stand it. Makes me sick every time."

"We fat all things to fat ourselves," I said.

"Your worm is your emperor of diet," Corsetti said.

I looked at him. He grinned.

"Shakespeare's a hobby," he said. "Lotta oddballs on the New York cops."

I nodded. "Assume it was Rambeaux," I said. "It's nearly a week since I talked with Perry Lehman at the Crown Prince Club. How long you figure Rambeaux's been dead?"

" 'Bout a week," Corsetti said. "Depends on how warm it was in there, but it's been a while."

"And it's sort of a coincidence that a hooker gets killed and then her pimp gets killed."

"And both of them have talked with a private cop from Boston first," Corsetti said.

"Be logical to have him as a suspect," I said.

"Would in fact," Corsetti said.

"All I'm trying to do is find a kid named April Kyle," I said.

"So you keep telling me," Corsetti said. "Now I've got two stiffs and no suspect except you."

"You don't think I did it," I said.

Corsetti shook his head. "No," he said. "Boston says you're clean, though annoying. I believe it. You got no reason to ace Rambeaux and then come back a week later and discover the body and call 911." A young woman in a ponytail wearing white shorts and blue running shoes went by. Corsetti looked after her. Her shorts were so high that the cheeks of her buttocks showed. Corsetti shook his head.

"So where are we?" he said.

"I don't know," I said. "Perry Lehman's got to be in this thing, and he's got mob connections in Boston. And he or they or somebody is killing people I talk to about April."

"Maybe," Corsetti said, "or maybe there's a whole other thing going on that you got nothing to do with."

"Assuming that doesn't leave me anything to do," I said.

"Readiness is all," Corsetti said.

"Not enough," I said.

"Might have to be," Corsetti said.

"No," I said. "Doesn't help me find April Kyle."

"For crissake," Corsetti said. "You were a cop. Hookers get clipped. So do pimps. Most of the time you don't know why and most people don't care why. How much time you think the city of New York wants me to spend on this thing?"

"Less than this," I said.

"That's right."

"But I work for a client who does want me to spend time," I said. "It's the luxury of the private sector."

"Most of the private sector is doing divorce tails and store security," Corsetti said.

I shrugged.

"You come across anything that might be useful to me, give me a call," Corsetti said. He handed me a card.

"You going to spend more time on this thing?" I said.

"You're going to spend time on it," Corsetti said, "I'm going to be ready."

"Okay," I said.

27

I had followed the string as far back as I could and it stopped dead at Perry Lehman. It didn't mean Lehman had done anything I cared about. It didn't mean that he could help me find April Kyle. It just meant that I didn't have anywhere else to look. So I decided to look at him some more.

It was full summer in Boston and the heat sat on the city like a possessive parent. I parked half up on the sidewalk near the corner of the alley that led to the Crown Prince Club, and got out and leaned on the fender with my arms folded. I had on a summer silk tweed jacket and a black polo shirt and jeans and running shoes. The jacket was to cover my gun. Summer weight or no, it was too hot for comfort; one of the drawbacks to being armed and dangerous in summer. I thought about getting back in the car and using the AC. But I wanted to be conspicuous. Sitting in the car would make me less so.

Nothing happened. After a half hour I took off my jacket. The gun made me even more conspicuous. But I had a permit and if it bothered people that wasn't my problem. It was nine-thirty in the morning.

Two guys looking a little blurry came out of the club and walked up the alley past me. One of them saw me and the gun and looked quickly away. He murmured something to his friend. They moved away up the alley toward Boylston Street and I caught one of them glancing back as he rounded the corner. At ten-fifteen a guy in a seersucker suit and a straw hat with a colorful band came down the alley and looked at me, and stopped and looked at his watch and looked at me covertly while he was looking at his watch and hesitated and then rang the bell at the Crown Prince Club and went in. At ten-forty another guy came down the alley and saw me and stopped and started forward and stopped and turned on his heel and went back up the alley. The lunch crowd began drifting down the alley at eleven-thirty, all men, rep ties and pin collars and briefcases and Bally shoes and suits from Louis. Many of the lunchers paid me no mind. But some did, and I made them uneasy.

My shirt was soaked through in back by twelve-fifteen when the big doorman in his Rudolf Friml uniform came out of the club and walked across the street. He was studiously uninterested in my gun.

"Miss Coolidge has asked me to see what it is you might want," the doorman said.

"I don't want anything," I said. "But thank Miss Coolidge anyway."

"Miss Coolidge doesn't like you standing out here wearing a gun looking at the members. Members don't like it much neither."

"I don't blame them," I said. "How'd you like to be caught walking into this place for lunch."

"Miss Coolidge asked me to ask you to move along."

"No," I said.

The doorman looked at me for a full thirty seconds.

"Gun buys you a little something," he said. "But don't count too heavy on it."

"You don't think Miss Coolidge will be satisfied with my response?"

"Don't seem likely," he said, and turned and walked back into the club.

It was quiet again, except for the sound of the sweat soaking into my shirt. People came and went from the Crown Prince Club. I thought about lunch. Maybe a lobster roll, and a draft beer. Two drafts, the moisture condensing on the side of the cold glass. And maybe a second lobster roll, but then I wouldn't come out even, so I'd have to have at least one more beer. By two o'clock the lunch traffic had dwindled to a precious few. I was thinking about the different ways beer could be chilled, and which way was most effective, when a maroon Oldsmobile sedan pulled down the alley past me and pulled to the side. Two guys got out and walked toward me. They were both dark-haired and wore thick mustaches. They might have been brothers. The one that got out the driver's side had a sunburned face and his nose was peeling. He had on a madras plaid sport coat with green predominant and a yellow V-neck T-shirt. His hair was combed smoothly back from his forehead and he had on thick-rimmed Ray-Ban sunglasses. His partner was maybe half an inch taller, his hair curled, wearing a Hawaiian shirt hanging out over his belt. Around his neck was a thick gold chain with an Italian pepper hanging from it. I could see by the way the shirt hung that he was wearing a gun under it.

The guy with the sunburned nose said, "What's happening, *chico?*"

I said, "Are you guys brothers?"

"Yeah, why?"

"I just wondered," I said. "Did you get your hair straightened or did he get a perm?"

"Funny," the guy with the sunburn said.

Curly said, "Don't fuck around with him, Paulie. It's hot, let's get him the fuck out of here and get back in the car."

Sunburn nodded. "He's right, *chico.* Let's hear it, what are you doing standing out here looking at the club?"

"You guys work for the club?" I said.

"We're asking the questions, *chico,* and we're getting tired of it. What are you doing here?"

"I'm staying in the sun," I said, "trying to get my nose to peel like yours. It's cute as a button."

"Okay, pal," Curly said, "enough. You either haul your ass out of here now, or we drop you right here on the street."

"Eek," I said.

"You don't think we'll do it?"

"I'm not sure you can," I said. "There's only two of you."

"Listen, stupid," the guy with the sunburn said, "you don't know who you're dealing with. You are getting yourself in really bad trouble."

"Who am I dealing with?" I said.

"You'll find out—if you don't smarten up."

"Listen," I said. "This is getting boring. You guys are stuck. They sent you over here to run me off but they told you not to make any trouble. So you can threaten me, but you can't back it up, because you were told not to."

"You think so, huh?"

"Jesus, who writes your dialogue? Yeah, I think so. The point here is to get me to stop causing trouble here, not to escalate it."

"Say that's right," Curly said. "That don't mean that you ain't going to run into trouble someplace else, if you get my drift."

"Yeah, that's occurred to me. But see, you think I'm

scared of you. You're used to it. Most people are scared of you. 'Cause you're official badasses, and you walk around with guns, and call people *chico.* What you don't under stand is that you should be scared of me."

The three of us stood there silently. Then the guy with the sunburn jerked his head at his brother and they turned and walked back to the Olds.

"You'll see us again," he said, and got in the car. The engine cranked and the car backed up with a lot of engine noise and tire squealing. I waved good-bye as it backed into Boylston Street and pulled away. When they were gone I walked up to the corner and found a pay phone in a drugstore and called Henry Cimoli at the Harbor Health Club.

"I need Hawk," I said. "I'm hanging around outside the Crown Prince Club, you know where that is?"

"Yeah, I know. It's a whorehouse for Yuppies," Henry said.

"Unkind," I said.

"But true," Henry said. "I'll tell him."

I bought a package of peanut butter Nabs at the check-out counter and went back down the alley and leaned against my car some more and ate the Nabs.

At five-ten Hawk parked behind me in the alley and got out and walked over to me. He had on a pale lavender sport jacket over a pink tank top. His slacks were creamy linen and his shoes off-gray. He had on wraparound sunglasses and his head gleamed in the late afternoon sun.

"You been here all day trying to get up courage to go in the Crown Prince Club," Hawk said. "And you want me to walk you over."

"I been standing here all day," I said, "and first the doorman came over and asked me to leave, and then two gunnies came around and told me to leave."

"You still here," Hawk said.

"Yeah, but I think maybe I need someone to keep an eye on my back."

"Who the gunnies?" Hawk said.

"Don't know. They were maybe thirty, brothers, southern European, one of them called the other one Paulie."

"Well, we know Perry Lehman connected."

"Yep."

"How come you standing around out here annoying everybody?" Hawk said.

"I don't know what else to do," I said. "So I figured if I annoyed Lehman enough maybe something would happen and I'd know what to do."

"You good at annoying," Hawk said.

"Years of study," I said.

"Yeah," Hawk said, "but you had a natural talent to start with."

28

At about a quarter to six, Perry Lehman came out of the Crown Prince Club. The doorman came with him. The doorman opened the door of a stretch limo, Perry got in and the stretch limo pulled away. I got in my car and followed it. We turned left onto Boylston and right onto Charles and left onto Beacon and headed west. The traffic was still heavy and the limo didn't go fast. There were a lot of stops. It wasn't hard to follow Lehman, but I wanted him to see me following, and with heavy traffic it took some doing. At six thirty-five the limo pulled into a long, curving drive in Chestnut Hill near the reservoir. I went right in behind it. The drive curved up among flowering shrubs and green lawn. The limo stopped under a portico in front of an enormous white château-style home. I pulled up behind it. A black man in a light gray three-piece suit came out to open the door, and another one came out dressed the same and stood beside the limo and looked at my car.

Lehman got out of the limo and turned and stared at me. The guy holding the door closed it and the limo pulled away. I sat in my car and looked back at Lehman. He said something to the two attendants and they all looked at me. Then the two black guys came over to my car.

"Mr. Lehman wishes to know what you want."

"Awful warm for a vest, isn't it?" I said.

"State your business, please."

"Actually I'm with the National Organization for Women, and I was wondering if Mr. Lehman would care to express himself on sexism in the marketplace."

The two men looked at each other.

"Equal pay for equal worth?" I said.

The guy talking to me had a small vertical scar on his upper lip. He turned toward Lehman.

"He's talking shit, Mr. Lehman, you want us to get hold of him?"

Lehman didn't move any closer. "I want him to get the fuck out of here and leave me alone," he said.

"You hear the man?"

"Tell him I can't hear him from so far away," I said. "Tell him to come closer."

The other guard said, "Man, you're crazy. You fighting to get yourself hurt."

"Get him out of here," Lehman said. His voice had risen slightly.

I yelled out the window of my car, "Hey, Perry, who's Warren?"

"Huh?"

"Ginger Buckey went to St. Thomas with Warren and ditched him and took off with a musician. Who's Warren?"

"Get him out of here." Lehman's voice was higher. "Now, get rid of him, I don't care how you do it."

"Drive off," said the guard with the scar, "or we drive it off for you with you in the trunk."

I put the car in gear and rolled on around the driveway. Slowly. Lehman had backed up into the front doorway. As I went by he said, "You're going to get yourself killed." His voice was high and shaky. "You're going to get killed."

I made a small V sign at him and drove on down the drive and parked out on Beacon Street opposite the driveway with the motor running. My old Subaru had given out after 126,000 miles and I had a new one, a turbo coupe with four-wheel drive. The turbo meant it would go pretty fast, and if I had to thwart a villain during inclement weather I could put it into four-wheel drive. Right now going fast seemed more important. The two bodyguards walked down to the end of the drive and looked at me parked across the street. I shot at them with my forefinger. And smiled. The guy with the scar said something to his buddy, the buddy looked at me and said something back to the guy with the scar. He shook his head and they stood and looked at me. I looked back. We did that until it got dark and I got tired and the gas gauge began to get low on the idling car and I put it in gear and turboed off to bed.

The next morning I was out front of Perry Lehman's house. I had a large cardboard placard nailed to a piece of 1 by 2 that I jammed into the ground near the end of his driveway. The placard said WHO'S WARREN? It was almost ten o'clock in the morning before Perry came down the driveway in his limo. The limo stopped by the sign and the chauffeur, in the same three-piece gray suit that the bodyguards wore, got out and pulled the sign out of the ground. He went around to the trunk and opened it, put the sign in and closed the trunk and came around to the front and spotted me and leaned back inside to speak to Lehman. Then he got in the car. The car sat motionless in the driveway for maybe five minutes before the two gray-suited bodyguards appeared. They looked across the street at me. I waited. They got in the limo. The guy with the scarred lip got in back with Lehman. The other got in the front with the driver. *I must be making an impression, three bodyguards. How flattering.*

Off we went toward Boston. It took only about fifteen minutes, outside of rush hour. When the limo pulled into the alley in front of the club, the two bodyguards got out first. I stopped well up the alley. It was getting to where they'd assault me on this and I wasn't ready for that yet. I wanted to keep pressuring Lehman until he did something profoundly stupid that might prove useful to me. I trusted him to do that if I had enough time.

With the guards watching me Lehman got out and walked to the club. There was a sign posted on the wall by the door. It said WHO'S WARREN? Lehman tore it off and went into the building. The bodyguards got back in the limo and it pulled away down the alley and made a U-turn. I backed into the street and pulled away first. I turned right on Boylston and right on Tremont and went around the block. The limo didn't chase me. I came through Park Square and back onto Boylston and pulled in and parked at the edge of the alley, and took residence on my front fender again. A few customers came and went. Some noticed me. At about noon I went up to the corner and called the Crown Prince Club and asked for Perry Lehman.

"Who's calling, please?"

"My name is Spenser."

"One moment, please."

Then Lehman's voice, sounding stiff and edgy. "What the fuck is this, Spenser?"

"I was wondering if you could help me, Perry."

"I'll help you, I'll help you right into the fucking ground," he said. "You think you can fuck with me like this? You're fucking with the wrong dude, pal, lemme tell you that."

"Gee, Perry, all I wanted to know was if you happened to know a guy named Warren, member of the club. . . ."

Lehman hung up.

I went back to the corner and leaned against my car some more and looked at the Crown Prince Club and let the Crown Prince Club look at me. Since yesterday when I talked with him I hadn't laid eyes on Hawk. I hadn't been looking for him, but it was still as puzzling as it always was that a guy as visible as Hawk could become entirely invisible whenever he needed to. Maybe he was really Lamont Cranston.

Perry must have decided to wait me out because for the rest of the day I was undisturbed. When the limo came to pick Lehman up in the late afternoon they paid me no mind. Lehman got in without even looking. The doorman when he opened the door ignored me and the two bodyguards did the same. They got out and flanked the car and never once glanced my way. Then they got in and the limo went to Chestnut Hill with me behind it.

I didn't go into the drive. I was trying to fine-tune this just short of violent confrontation. So I parked out on

Beacon Street again, and nobody came and looked at me until it got dark and I went home.

Rejection.

The next day I went through the routine. At noon that day Lehman got a telegram inquiring about Warren, and at four that afternoon a special delivery letter came for Warren, c/o The Crown Prince Club. I continued to be ignored. Perry's people were big aggressive guys but they weren't shooters. That kind of trouble would come from the people who owned Perry. It was getting toward the time when I figured it would come, and I wanted it to come. I needed to have a run-in with the pros and win, before I took my next step. I didn't have a plan exactly but I had some sort of inchoate sense of where I wanted this to go. It was much more than I was used to having.

29

The pros appeared on Monday afternoon as I was following Perry home. A brown Dodge sedan stayed two or three cars behind me out Beacon Street to Chestnut Hill. They did a decent tail job, but it's hard, with one car, to tail a guy who's expecting it. Lehman's limo swung into his driveway and I parked on the street in front. The Dodge turned off into a side street before it reached me. They wouldn't hit me outside Lehman's house. I sat for a while and thought about where I wanted them to hit me. Someplace where Hawk would have room to operate, somewhere that had open space so I could see them coming before they got in range.

I put the Subaru in gear and U-turned and headed back down Beacon Street to Chestnut Hill Avenue. I drove at an easy speed out Chestnut Hill Ave. through Brighton to Soldiers Field Road, along the Charles River near the Public Theater. The river in this section was bordered with open parkland, punctuated by hot-topped parking areas. People picnicked here and launched boats and walked dogs and jogged and threw Frisbees and rode bicycles. Across the river Watertown merged with Cambridge and on my side the road curved on past Harvard Stadium and became Storrow Drive.

I got out of the car and looked aimlessly around the area. It was not crowded, most people were eating supper. The commuter traffic heading out toward Newton was thinning. I had my gun out and held it at my side hidden behind the car. It was heavy artillery for me. An S&W .357 magnum in case one of the hit men was a Cape buffalo. The brown Dodge came into the parking area and I moved down toward the front of my car for a better look at the water. Whichever side they came on I could move to the other. The Dodge swung in on the driver's side of the Subaru and parked. Without looking at it I moved a couple of steps around to the other side of my car, staying near the front where the engine made a better shield than the passenger compartment. The driver and two other guys got out. I hadn't seen any of them before. One of them went to the trunk and opened it, and two others looked across the river at the apartment building being completed. Hawk's white Jaguar pulled in off the roadway and pulled in beside the Dodge. The guy at the trunk stared at it and then looked toward me. I moved another step behind the car. The two gunnies near the front of the car produced handguns and began to move around my car toward me. The guy at the trunk produced a double-barreled shotgun and stepped toward the rear of my car. I crouched.

Hawk stepped out of his Jag with a .12-gauge pump and hit the guy with the double-barrel a horizontal butt stroke on the back of his head. He went down, the double-barreled shotgun went sliding along the ground toward me and Hawk leaned over the roof of the Dodge and pointed the pump gun at the two gunnies in front.

"Y'all freeze," he said.

The two handguns stopped still, I straightened up behind the Subaru and pointed my gun at them. The lead gunnie turned his head carefully and stared at Hawk.

"Howdy doo," Hawk said. And smiled kindly.

I said, "Take the piece by the barrel, with your left hand, and throw it in the river. You, with the hat, do it first."

The guy with the Red Sox baseball hat tossed his gun in the river.

The guy Hawk had decked made a groaning noise and shifted from facedown to his side. The second gunnie threw his piece into the Charles. Hawk walked over behind the Subaru and picked up the double-barrel. He started to throw it in the river, and stopped and looked at it a moment. Then he gave an approving nod and walked to his Jaguar. He opened the trunk and put the shotgun in and closed the trunk and locked it.

"Nice weapon," he said.

"Lie facedown on the ground," I said to the two shooters. "Hands behind your head."

They did it. The shotgun man was on his hands and knees. I reached down and helped him to his feet. He was frowning with pain.

"What's your name?" I said.

"Bernie," he said.

" 'My Attorney, Bernie,' " I said.

"Huh?"

"It's a Dave Frishberg song," I said.

"We were just going to warn you," Bernie said.

"Un huh."

"We weren't going to clip you, man. Ask them." He gestured at the two men on the ground. "We were just supposed to tell you to lay off."

"And you was planning to speak to him through the shotgun," Hawk said, "which was why you was pointing it at him."

"Who sent you?" I said. "I know it's a corny question, but I can't think of how else to ask."

"Just a guy," Bernie said. "Guy I don't know. Just said he wanted you told to stop bothering Mr. Lehman."

"Honest to God?" I said. "Probably ran into him at the Athenaeum while you were researching Increase Mather."

"Just met him in a bar, is all," Bernie said.

I slapped him with my open left hand full across the face. It rocked him and he took a step back and then steadied himself, blinking his eyes and staring at me. His headache must have been a starburst.

"Who was it sent you?" I said.

"Hey, man, shit," Bernie said. And I rattled his head with another openhanded slap.

"Better tell him," Hawk said, " 'fore you make him mad."

Bernie shook his head and stopped with half a shake. I put the gun under my arm and slapped him left hand right hand left hand right hand as hard and as fast as I could. He got his hands up and protected his face. So I slapped him on the side of the head, keeping the pace. When he moved his hands to protect his head, I slapped his face.

"They'll, they'll . . . they'll kill me," he said.

I stopped.

Bernie had his eyes clenched shut. He nodded, his face red from the slapping. His lip was bleeding.

"They'll find out," he said. His eyes still shut, he dropped his hands a little farther and I slapped him again.

"Stop it, man, stop it," he said.

"Who sent you," I said. "You tell me and you walk away."

Hawk said, "You getting tired? Want me to hit him awhile?"

"Another couple of minutes," I said.

"Jacky Wax," Bernie said.

I looked at Hawk. "John Weatherwax," I said.

Hawk said, "Un huh. Which means Mr. Milo."

"Well," I said, "aren't we in the big leagues."

Hawk nodded. "Funny they send people from the farm system," he said.

"I'm offended," I said.

"Don't blame you," Hawk said. "Want me to shoot them?"

"No," I said, "not this time. I want them to go tell Jacky Wax to tell Mr. Milo that I want to know who Warren is and it might be easier if somebody just told me."

"They know I told they'll kill me," Bernie said.

"Phrase it any way you like," I said. "Hit the ground."

Bernie got prone beside his helpers.

I reached into my car and came out with a newly purchased can of Krylon maroon spray paint. I carefully spray-painted the hair of the two shooters.

"Be interesting," I said to Hawk, "to hear them explain this one."

"Punk," Hawk said. "They can claim they going punk."

"They did that long ago," I said.

Hawk went and got in his Jag. He pressed a button and the windows rolled down silently.

"Maybe next time they send major leaguers," he said.

"Should I get a different color paint?" I said.

Hawk chuckled. "Increase Mather?" he said.

"Hell," I said, "he's easy. How about 'My Attorney, Bernie'?"

Hawk eased the Jag into gear.

"Never knew somebody knew more stuff that didn't matter," he said. He backed the Jaguar out.

"What else is there to know," I said. But Hawk was already rolling and didn't hear me.

I followed him.

30

The next morning Hawk and I went to see Perry Lehman.

"Tell Mr. Lehman that I need to talk," I told the doorman. "I'm sure we can straighten this out."

The doorman went inside. When he came back out he said, "Miss Coolidge says she'll see you."

"It's a start," I said.

Hawk was looking at the doorman without expression, but in the blank and placid gaze there was somehow amusement. The doorman felt it and looked at Hawk.

"Fine threads," Hawk said.

The doorman opened the door and we went in. Same oak waiting room, same decanter of port. Gretchen Coolidge was waiting for us.

"What is it you wish?" she said.

"This is my associate, Hawk," I said. "Hawk, this is Gretchen Coolidge."

Hawk nodded and smiled.

Gretchen said, "How do you do," and then turned toward me and said, "What is it you want now?" and then made a tiny sideways flicker of a glance at Hawk.

"I'm hoping for rapprochement," I said.

"Oh, really?"

"Yes, I have compelling evidence that Perry Lehman's life is in danger and I need to warn him of it and suggest a solution."

"Mr. Spenser," she said, "what on earth are you trying to do now?"

"Gretchen," I said, "observe this face. Look at these wide-spaced intelligent eyes. Is this a man who would deceive you?"

"Or could," Hawk murmured.

I ignored him. Gretchen gave him another covert eye flicker.

"Mr. Spenser. We are trying to run an honest business here. You have disrupted that with threats and intimidation on behalf of God knows who or what and driven Mr. Lehman and myself to near distraction. Now you want me to believe that you can prevent the execution of a death threat on the same person you've been harassing?"

"Distraction?" I said. "By golly, that's pretty good. I had hoped at best for annoyance, but distraction . . ." I whistled silently.

"I don't find any of this funny," Gretchen said.

"Lot of people tell me that," I said. "But this is on the level. The way things are developing there's a very real risk to Mr. Lehman."

She stared at me for a moment.

Hawk said, "This business so legitimate, how come when Spenser start harassing you you don't call the cops."

"Our membership is entitled to privacy and not to police and press presence, Mr., ah, Hawk."

Hawk nodded. " 'Course," he said, and smiled at her.

She held her gaze on him for a moment and then turned her face sharply back at me.

"This is probably another harassment ploy," she said.

I didn't say anything.

"But I cannot take it upon myself to dismiss it as such, as no doubt you fully anticipated. May I have the details before I inform Mr. Lehman?"

I shook my head. "I don't think Perry would like me telling anyone but him the details."

She tightened her lips. "Of course," she said. "Again it's a ploy I can't really reject." She took a deep breath and let it out. "I'm afraid you've forced my hand, Mr. Spenser. Please have a seat while I inform Mr. Lehman."

She turned and went out through the big oaken door opposite the entrance. Hawk and I declined a seat and stood alone in the waiting room.

"Businesslike," Hawk said.

"Yes," I said, "she's very professional."

"Lots of professionals here," Hawk said.

"Sort of," I said.

"We gonna paint Perry's head or what," Hawk said.

"I'm going to outwit him," I said. "And while I am you're going to keep the Royal African bodyguard from kicking me to death."

"The brother at the door did look dandy in his costume," Hawk said.

"They all do," I said. "Neocolonial chic."

"Embarrassing," Hawk said.

It was maybe ten minutes before Gretchen came back and told us we could see Perry Lehman. In the elevator I caught her peeking at Hawk sideways out of a narrow corner of her right eye.

Lehman was in his rooftop garden. Near him Charles Jackson was standing at parade rest, in uniform. There were two other security attendants across the pool. Hawk took it in as we walked toward Lehman's desk and gave me his expressionless look of amusement.

"You think a mechanical hippo gonna come out of that pool and scare us?" he said.

Lehman was sitting behind his desk. Not lounging.

"Don't try anything," he said. "I'm telling you right now there's three men here and I can get a dozen more in thirty seconds. So don't try a single thing, you understand?" There was a glass of champagne half drunk beside him, a bottle in the silver ice bucket near his desk. Jackson showed no flicker of recognition or connection.

I said, "Perry we came to help you, not hurt you."

"You're trying to help me right out of fucking business," he said. "What's this shit about my life being in danger?"

"Miss Manners have a contract out on you," Hawk said.

Charles Jackson's face moved slightly as if it wanted to smile and then went back into its stony palace-guard mask.

"What'd he say?" Lehman spoke to me. He didn't look at Hawk.

"We need to talk, Perry. You mind the guards hearing what we say?"

"I'm not giving up my guards," he said. His hand hovered near the corner of his desk. Probably the panic button for the other dozen men.

"Okay," I said. I sat down in one of the chairs near the desk and crossed my legs. Relaxed, nonthreatening.

Gretchen was standing to Lehman's right. Now that the focus had shifted she was looking more openly at Hawk.

"Or Miss Coolidge?" I said.

"Stop fucking around," Lehman said. "You got something to say, say it and then haul your ass out of here."

"Asses," I said. "There's two of us."

"What is it?"

"Yesterday some of the heavy hitters came after me. Three guys working for Jacky Wax, who, as we all know, is with Mr. Milo."

"I don't know nothing about any of that."

"Doubtless," I said. "Anyway, they were not heavy-enough hitters. With the help of my associate"—I nodded at Hawk. He smiled modestly—"I was able to thwart them and send them back to Jacky with their hair painted maroon."

Jackson had trouble with his face again.

Lehman said, "What? What the fuck you talking about?"

"Your owners tried to hit me to keep me from looking into Warren, and they failed badly."

"I told you, I don't know anything about that. What's it got to do with me being in danger." Lehman drank more champagne. When he put the glass down, Jackson stepped forward and filled it for him.

"Well, think about it for a minute, Perry. Somebody very badly doesn't want me to find out about old Warren."

"I don't know any fucking Warren," Lehman said.

"Of course not," I said. "But if you did, then the people who didn't want me to find out about Warren could think about going two ways."

Lehman frowned and drank his champagne and

looked at Gretchen Coolidge. "Guy's crazy, Gretch, guy's off his fucking nut, you know?"

Gretchen nodded.

"They could kill me," I said. "Which would be very effective. But they've tried and it worked out badly for them. Doesn't mean they won't try again, but my associate and I are a hard nut to crack and they may choose to crack an easier one."

"Meaning?"

"Meaning maybe they'll kill you."

Lehman opened his mouth and closed it without speaking.

"And Miss Coolidge," I said.

Gretchen's expression didn't change. Lehman looked quickly at Charles Jackson.

"See how it would work?" I said. "Just pretend for a minute Mr. Milo doesn't want me to know who Warren is, and he's having trouble getting me to stop asking. If he clips you and Miss Coolidge I got no one left to ask. He doesn't have to make me stop."

The faint sound of the pool filter was all that broke the silence in the room. I looked at Lehman. Hawk looked at nothing. Charles Jackson looked at Hawk. He didn't seem afraid of Hawk, which was a mistake.

Lehman picked up his champagne glass and emptied it and put it down. He jerked his head toward the door.

"Out," he said. "You said what you had to say, now take a hike."

"Hard as nails," I said to Hawk.

"Tough as a nickel steak," Hawk said.

Lehman waggled his thumb toward the door.

"Go on," he said, "walk out of here while you still can."

"Don't say I didn't warn you," I said.

Hawk glanced at me, and then turned, as I did, and walked toward the door.

"Show them out, Gretch," Lehman said. "You two go with her." He gestured to the men across the pool. "Make sure the nosy bastards aren't snooping around in here."

Charles Jackson poured more champagne in Lehman's glass.

"Nosy bastards," Lehman said.

Gretchen Coolidge opened the door and we went out. The two guards came behind us and Gretchen brought up the rear. No one said anything until we got to the front door.

"Ms. Coolidge," I said, "believe me, I don't want to see anyone get hurt. If you know something tell me now, before it's too late."

Her face was stiff and her movements angular.

"Good day, Mr. Spenser," she said, and nodded at Hawk, and closed the door and we went out.

" 'Don't say I didn't warn you'?" Hawk said.

I shrugged.

" 'Tell me now 'fore it too late'?" he said.

"So I was a little schmaltzy," I said.

"Schmaltzy," Hawk said. "Man, you embarrassing me in front of the brothers."

"They're not schmaltzy?" I said.

"Good point," Hawk said. "How long you think he hold on 'fore he panic?"

"Hard to say," I said. "If he doesn't panic quickly we'll go to plan B."

"Plan B," Hawk said. "Man, you a high-tech thug."

31

Lehman was tougher or slower or more full of illusion than I had thought. We waited three days and he didn't do anything to help us, so we went to plan B.

Hawk came up with a late-model Cadillac sedan with doctored plates. I didn't ask him where he got it and he didn't say. We drove it out to Chestnut Hill and parked it at the foot of Lehman's drive. We both wore ski masks. Hawk was in the driver's seat. I was in back with the windows down, and when Lehman's limousine slowed to turn into his yard I put my Smith & Wesson pump out the window and blasted three rounds of #6 birdshot into the trunk and rear panel of the limo. Then Hawk slipped the Caddy into gear and we drove off.

The birdshot would mess up the paint and scare Lehman without much risk of killing anybody and unless he knew more about pellet weight and muzzle velocity than I thought he did, he'd think someone tried to do him in.

We left the Cadillac in the parking garage near Filene's in the Chestnut Hill Mall and climbed into my Subaru and headed back to Boston. To await developments. When we got to my office the developments had arrived already. There was a message on my answering machine that said I should call Perry Lehman whenever I got in, no matter what time. I could call him at his home or at the club, and both private numbers were on the tape.

"Perry sound a little shaky," Hawk said.

"If you thought Mr. Milo was having you killed wouldn't you be a little shaky?" I said.

"No," Hawk said.

"True," I said. "I withdraw the question."

" 'Sides," Hawk said, "I believe Mr. Milo is in fact trying to have you killed. You shaky?"

"Only when no one's looking," I said.

I dialed Lehman's home number. He answered himself.

"Spenser," I said. "You called?"

"Jesus Christ, Spenser. They did it. They tried to hit me, all over a fucking banker, for crissake. It's a banker, named Warren Whitfield."

"You okay?" I said.

"Yeah, they missed, but you gotta let Mr. Milo know, Spenser. You gotta tell him you know it's Warren Whitfield."

"Then he'll try to kill me instead of you," I said.

"Man, it was your idea. You know how to do this kind of shit."

"What bank does Warren work for?" I said.

"He don't work for a bank, for crissake, he's the president. DePaul Federal. You gotta tell Mr. Milo."

"And tell him how I know?"

"Jesus, no, for fuck sake, why do you want to kill me?"

"Okay," I said, "then you just sit tight and in a while the pressure will be off."

"What are you going to do?"

"Sit tight," I said, and hung up.

Almost immediately the phone rang again. I took it off the hook and broke the connection and left it off the hook. I looked at Hawk. "Warren Whitfield," I said. "President of DePaul Federal."

"Told you we in the bigs," Hawk said.

"We are in fact," I said.

"Now what," Hawk said.

"I suppose we got to talk with Warren," I said. "Ask him about Ginger, ask him if he knows where April is."

"You wonder why Mr. Milo's interested in protecting the president of a bank," Hawk said.

"They're both capitalists," I said.

"You awful cynical for a romantic," Hawk said.

"I'm not romantic about Mr. Milo," I said.

"Glad there's something," Hawk said.

Hawk went home. And I sat at my desk for a while

with my feet up. The desk lamp was on but the rest of the office was dim. Outside, the Back Bay was quiet. And the light from the street was muted by the time it reached the window. I'd been following the sad track of a dead girl for too long. And the dead girl wasn't even who I was looking for. Maybe April was dead too. Maybe I'd been following a dead girl to find a dead girl. I looked at the backs of my hands. A couple of the knuckles on my left hand had been broken and healed a little larger. The hands were real, though, flesh and blood, alive. The pimp was dead too. Which pimp, I'd met so many lately. Rambeaux, the late Robert Rambeaux, reed man. Maybe they were all either pimps or whores. Maybe it was life's classifying principle, maybe I had seen the eternal Footman hold my coat, and snicker.

I called Susan at home.

"I'm sitting in my office with only one light on," I said, "and I'm quoting Prufrock to myself."

"My God," she said, "tell me about it."

"Everybody I run into looking for April is a pimp," I said. "Except for the whores."

"Everybody?"

"Metaphorically at least. It's depressing."

"The last time you found her she went right back to whoring," Susan said.

"Yeah, that's not encouraging either. What kind of world is it when whoring is the best choice open to you?"

"Since when do you and I talk about the world," she said. "The world is what it is."

"Yeah, I know."

"Not only do you know, you've helped me to know."

"Good to be useful," I said.

"What has always made me respect you, even in the bad times, was your ability to look out at the world and see what's there. Not what you'd like to see, or even what you need to see, but simply what's there."

"I haven't killed anyone yet this trip."

Susan was silent for a moment on the phone, then she said, "Ah, that's what it is. It's not this, it's still San Francisco.

"And Idaho," she said.

"Whatever you did, and whoever you killed, and however you feel about it, you have to judge all of that in context. You were doing what you felt you had to do, and you were doing it for love."

"The people I killed are just as dead."

"Yes. It makes no difference to them why you did it. But it makes a difference to me and to you. What we've been through in the last couple of years has produced the relationship we have now, achieved love, maybe. Something we've earned, something we've paid for in effort and pain and maybe mistakes as well. I live with some."

"I know," I said.

"We aren't who we were," she said.

"I know," I said.

"But if you are to continue what you do you cannot be afraid to kill someone if you must. Otherwise you'll die and if you do some of me will die as well."

"I know," I said.

"So either come to terms with that or do something else. We almost lost each other once."

"Doing something else doesn't seem too swell," I said.

"No, it doesn't. You are the best there is at what you do. And what you do is often crucially important to someone."

"You love me," I said, "don't you."

"More than I can say. Maybe more sometimes than I can show."

"Yes," I said, "I know."

"You want to come over?"

"No," I said, "I'm okay."

"You weren't when you called," Susan said.

"I am now," I said.

"No wonder I'm called super shrink," Susan said.

"Hey, wait a minute, the patient does all the work."

"Of course," Susan said. "You ought to not forget that

whoever you killed last year, there were people you could have killed and didn't."

"There's that," I said.

"We all do what we need to, and what we have to, not what we ought to, or ought to have. You're a violent man. You wouldn't do your work if you weren't. What makes you so attractive, among other things, is that your capacity for violence is never random, it is rarely self-indulgent, and you don't take it lightly. You make mistakes. But they are mistakes of judgment. They are not mistakes of the heart."

"I thought you shrinks didn't talk about heart."

"We only do it with the patients who aren't paying," she said.

"Thank you," I said.

"When will I see you?" Susan said.

"Maybe tomorrow night. I'll call you tomorrow."

"Okay, take care of yourself."

"Yes," I said.

We hung up. I sat silently in the office for ten minutes and then got up and turned off the light and went home.

32

I made three tries at getting Warren Whitfield on the phone next morning and never getting past the administrative assistant, who remained courteous and implacable no matter how beguiling I became. Finally I sent him a telegram that read:

> In regards Ginger Buckey, the Crown Prince Club, and St. Thomas, call Spenser, promptly.

I added my phone number and sat back to wait. He didn't call that day. And Hawk and I spent the time considering a number of pressing issues. We discussed whether ethnicity had anything to do with sexual fervor among women. We also examined the issue of why the Red Sox kept building teams around the long ball and the short left-field fence, a practice that had won them three pennants in the last forty years. I quoted Peter Gammons, Hawk referenced Bob Ryan, all four of us agreed. We analyzed the relative merits of California champagne. I opted for Schramsberg, he for Iron Horse. We agreed that Taittinger was the class of the French though Krug and Cristal and Dom Pérignon were worth a gulp. We agreed that Tapas Restaurant was the class of Porter Square, that Ray Robinson was the best fighter that ever lived (present company excluded), that Bill Russell was the most dominant basketball player, that Mel Tormé could sing; we spoke well of Picasso, and Alan Ameche and the Four Seasons. We engaged in a long sexist analysis of female physiology. At about four-thirty we turned on my answering machine and walked up the street to Grille Twenty-three and had a couple of beers at the bar. I called Susan and she said she'd meet us for supper. We had a couple more beers. The bar began to fill. The seat next to Hawk remained empty.

"You doing something," I said, "or is it racism?"

"Need a place for Susan," Hawk said.

"You're looking at people when they start to sit there," I said.

"Just a glance," Hawk said.

Susan arrived at a quarter to seven. As she came in she didn't do anything different than anyone else, but somehow she seemed to sweep in. There probably was no hush in the place. I probably imagined it. I always felt like a hush fell when she swept into a place. Hawk moved to the empty seat beside him and Susan sat between us. She kissed Hawk, and kissed me and gave me a hug with her right arm. She ordered a White Russian and looked at Hawk.

"I love you," she said, "but it always makes me nervous when I see you. It means he's into something too much for him to handle alone. Which means it's really too much."

"Maybe I into something I can't handle alone, Susan. Ever think of that?" Hawk said.

"No. Of course, it would work that way too," she said. "I guess I'm Spensocentric."

"Me too," I said. "Want me to get us a table?"

"Not yet," Susan said, "unless you're starving. I'd like to sit a little and come down."

"The crazies getting to you," I said.

"No, not really. I love what I do. And, mostly, I love the patients. But the concentration level is so high and so sustained that I am buzzed when I get through every night."

The bar was crowded now, people standing, mostly suits and ties after work at insurance companies. Police headquarters was right across the street but I didn't see much that looked like fuzz.

"How did you manage to save me a seat?" Susan said.

Hawk smiled. "Luck of the draw, Susan."

She studied him for a moment. "Maybe," she said.

Hawk and I finished our beer. Susan had a second White Russian. Then we went to dinner.

Grille Twenty-three occupied part of what used to be the Salada Tea Building. The building was from the era of vaulted ceilings and marble pillars, and the restaurant had made full use of the space. The dining room was separated from the bar by a railing and a couple steps down. Susan and Hawk and I sat near a display table of fresh produce and bread, which looked, somehow, better than it sounds. We got menus and Hawk took the wine list.

Susan said, "Tell me what you are doing now. I know you're still looking for April. But why Hawk?"

Hawk was absorbed in the wine list.

"Well, there was a mystery man named Warren," I said.

"Warren? What kind of name is Warren for a mystery man," Susan said.

"See why I was feeling Prufrockian?" I said.

"Go on," Susan said.

Hawk asked to see the wine steward. I told Susan about Perry Lehman and Warren and Mr. Milo. The wine steward conferred with Hawk, and went away.

"Schramsberg," Hawk said. "They didn't have Iron Horse. I was going to have one of each and do a blind tasting."

"After four or five beers," I said, "to prepare the palate."

Hawk grinned.

"And you knew Hawk would show up when they came to kill you?"

"Un huh."

"Even though you didn't see him and hadn't seen him all day?"

"Un huh."

"Isn't that remarkable," Susan said. "Have you each ever considered how rare that kind of trust is?"

"Yes," I said, "I have."

Hawk simply smiled at Susan.

"He doesn't consider stuff like that," I said.

She looked at Hawk.

"It have to do with us both knowing it matters," Hawk said. "Our line of work, you got to do what you say you going to do."

"See," Susan said, "he does think about such things."

"But not too much, Susan," Hawk said. "Doing it, more important than thinking about it."

The waiter brought the champagne. He opened it and poured. Susan ordered grilled salmon fillet. So did I. Hawk had scallops. We sipped the champagne. Susan's hand rested on mine on the tabletop. The room was full of the sound of people talking and dishes being served and steaks being cut and glasses being raised and fish being grilled and wine being poured. I looked at Susan, she smiled and said, "Umph," at me. We both knew what we were feeling. Since Hawk seemed to know whatever he felt like knowing, he probably knew it too.

"Nice to be dining with you both," Hawk said. He gestured slightly with the champagne glass and drank some. Susan and I drank some too.

"We've been together on worse occasions," I said.

"But few better," she said.

The food came. We had a platter of assorted grilled vegetables to go with our entrée. The waiter served some onto each plate. Susan smiled up at him when he finished. He poured more champagne and looked at Hawk. Hawk nodded and the waiter went for another bottle.

I said to Susan, "You keep smiling at the waiter that way and he's going to get vertigo and drop his tray and get fired."

"I forgot," Susan said, "I must control this special power."

"Smile at me," I said. "I'm so tough I can take the full force, ear to ear."

The waiter came back with a second bottle and leaned over Hawk. "Lady up there wants to buy you this next bottle, sir," the waiter said. He handed Hawk a business card on which something was written.

Hawk read the card and the message and looked up across the room at a tall blond woman in a tight-fitting red knit dress. He smiled once, and tucked the card into his shirt pocket.

"Your smile seems to be working pretty good too," I said.

"Thermonuclear," Hawk said.

"You know her?" Susan said.

"Not yet," Hawk said, and smiled again.

I put my hands lightly over Susan's eyes. "I know you love me," I said, "but there's no sense taking chances."

33

At nine-fifteen the next morning I got a call from Warren Whitfield's personal, senior, confidential assistant.

"Mr. Whitfield would like to have you stop by this morning at ten o'clock," she said.

"Be pleased to," I said.

"Thank you," she said.

DePaul Federal was about a half-hour walk from my office. With Hawk drifting along behind me on the other side of the street I set out at nine-thirty. I liked to walk and had been falling behind on my jogging lately, so the walk was especially welcome. The weather was about as good as summer gets as I headed down Boylston Street. Temperature eighty-one, sunny, small breeze.

The DePaul Building was forty-five stories with a high art deco lobby facing out on Franklin Street and Post Office Square. The cashiers and floor people occupied most of the floor, and a bank of elevators off a slightly raised walkway led to the executive offices up on top.

Hawk stayed in the lobby. No one was likely to hit me in the office of the man they'd been trying so hard to keep out of trouble. I found Whitfield's name on the directory and went to the thirty-seventh floor at a rate sufficient to make my ears block. I got out of the elevator, swallowing to clear my eustachian tubes. The foyer was deeply carpeted in banker's gray. Straight ahead was a large mahogany desk and a receptionist.

I said, "My name is Spenser. I have an appointment with Prez Whitfield."

"Yes, sir," she said with a lovely smile. "I'll tell him you're here."

She picked up the phone and punched a button. Her fingernails were painted a muted pink.

"Mr. Spenser is here," she said into the phone. Then she hung up. Almost at once the door behind her opened and a woman came out wearing a gray pinstripe suit and a white shirt with a ruffled bow at the collar.

"Mr. Spenser," she said. "Please come in."

I followed her. The skirt of her suit came just to the bend of her knee. She wore black pumps. We walked through another waiting room with a black oak desk in it and a woman sitting at it who wore dark maroon nail polish. I followed the pinstripe through one of a set of raised-panel oak doors into an office that looked out over Boston Harbor and south past Dorchester and the painted gas tanks along the Southeast Expressway. In front of the big windows a man sat at a bleached maple worktable, nearly bare of papers, with a phone bank near the left-hand corner, and a couple of manila folders stacked on the right. Against the left wall was another desk with a lot of papers and a similar phone bank and an empty black swivel chair with arms.

"Mr. Spenser," Pinstripe said, "Mr. Whitfield."

Whitfield rose but didn't put out a hand. I stood opposite him across the desk.

"I'll see Mr. Spenser alone, Helen," Whitfield said. He was looking steadily at me.

"Fine," Pinstripe said, and went out and closed the door.

Whitfield and I remained standing. He was a short man, and overweight. His hair was short and combed straight back and he had a clipped mustache that was sprinkled with gray. Dark suit, white shirt, yellow tie. Yellow was supposed to be the new power color.

Whitfield kept staring at me. His eyes were very pale blue and unblinking. The killer stare. I looked back. The office was silent. Everywhere money must have been being dispersed and collected and counted. But no sound of it reached the office. Whitfield pursed his lips silently, as if coming to a negative conclusion on my loan application. He looked some more.

"I'm getting bored," I said. "You want me to faint or anything?"

"Sit down," Whitfield said.

I sat in a mahogany chair upholstered in black leather. Whitfield went and sat in his high-backed leather swivel He leaned back slightly and folded his arms, still gazing at me. I waited.

There were paintings of sailing ships on the walls.

"What game are you playing?" Whitfield said.

"I'm trying to find April Kyle, and I'm trying to find out what happened to Ginger Buckey, and how come someone killed her?"

Whitfield made a short dismissive shake of his head. "I'm not concerned," he said, "with how you waste your time. When it's yours. I want to know what game you're playing with me."

"You knew Ginger Buckey," I said. "You took her to the Crown Prince resort in St. Thomas and she dumped you and went off with a reed man named Robert Rambeaux. He's dead too."

"If you make any such allegation before a witness," Whitfield said, "I will certainly sue you."

"Sure," I said. "But what I'd rather is that you tell me about Ginger, and maybe about April."

Whitfield slapped his open hand down on the desk. "Are you crazy?" he said. "Who the hell do you think you're talking to. You're looking for a couple of adolescent chippies and you come into my office and ask me? Do you have any idea what you're doing?"

"I didn't say they were chippies," I said.

Whitfield leaned forward over the desk, letting the swivel chair come forward with him.

"Don't play cute games with me, pal," he said.

"Warren," I said, "if you keep scaring me to death this is going to take all day. You think you're a powerful guy. You think it's because of something in you that you're powerful, so you figure to unleash a little of that power on me and watch me get limp and shriveled."

Whitfield's eyes were narrowed a little and both hands were flat on the top of the desk as he looked at me.

"But you're not a powerful guy," I said, "and what power you have isn't in you, it's in the job, in the fact that you control a lot of money and a lot of jobs and people want both, so they suck around. I don't want either. I want to know what you know about Ginger Buckey, and I'm going to find out."

Whitfield raised his hand. With the index finger extended he jabbed toward me with it. I kept right on talking.

"And until I find out," I said, "I'm going to be so annoying that it will make your eyes water."

"I don't know what you're talking about," Whitfield said. "I've been to the Crown Prince Club locally once or twice for lunch. I occasionally vacation in St. Thomas. But I don't know any Ginger Whatsis, or any April."

"Yeah you do," I said, "and you know Perry Lehman who runs the place and you know some other stuff that Mr. Milo doesn't want me to find out, and I want to know what that is too."

The name Mr. Milo rocked him. He sat back and some of the edge went off his voice.

"Mr. Milo?" he said.

"Un huh."

"Who's Mr. Milo?" he said.

I shook my head. "Come off it, Warren. We both know you know who Mr. Milo is. Even if you were clean, you'd know who Mr. Milo was."

He was back to looking at me again. But the look was fuzzier now.

"And I know that something is going down here between you and Mr. Milo because Mr. Milo has already tried to hit me after I started looking for you. The too-bad part for you, Warren, is that I'm probably going to knock the whole thing over, whereas if someone had told me about April Kyle back at the start, I wouldn't care much what you and Mr. Milo were doing."

"I . . ." Whitfield started to talk and stopped. On the right wall past the assistant's desk a door opened and

Jacky Wax walked through. He walked over to Whitfield's desk and punched one of the buttons on the phone.

"Jesus Christ," Whitfield said. "You can't show yourself here."

"Shut up," Jacky said without heat. He wasn't looking at Whitfield. He was looking at me.

"How's things, Jacky," I said.

"I don't think they're too good, right now," Jacky said, "especially for you."

He was a tall wiry guy with high shoulders. He was wearing an eight-hundred-dollar suit of pale gray, with a pink shirt and a pink-and-lavender striped tie. His pocket handkerchief was lavender-and-pink dots. His shoes were shiny black and long and pointy and probably cost nearly what the suit cost. He was wearing the kind of sunglasses that lighten inside and darken outside. His dark hair was cut long on top and short on the sides and combed back with a big wave in front and a part on the left side.

"Dammit, Jacky," Whitfield said, "I warned you to stay out of sight. Now he knows."

"He knows anyway," Jacky said. "He don't know any more than he did. And it's nothing he can prove."

I nodded. "He's right," I said to Whitfield. "I know you're connected to Mr. Milo. I know you went to St. Thomas with Ginger Buckey. And so far there's nothing I can prove. But there will be."

"No," Jacky said, "there won't. No need to be fancy about this. We're going to kill you." Jacky had no emotion in his voice. He might have been talking about real estate.

I was watching Whitfield. The talk was scaring him badly.

"Like I said, all I want is a kid named April Kyle, you clucks have been in a goddamned lather to keep me away from Whitfield when all I want is April Kyle, now you've got it escalated to where you've got to kill me."

"Don't make any difference," Jacky said, "how it got here, it's where we are. I'd have done it a long time ago, but I'm not in charge."

"How 'bout Warren?" I said. "He's looking a little peckish."

"He does what he's told," Jacky said. "And he likes it."

"You may have to do him too," I said. "I think the strain's getting to him."

"Don't matter none to me," Jacky said. "Won't matter much to you either, you being dead and all."

"God damn it, Jacky, I don't want this kind of thing talked about in here. It implicates me. Take this talk out into the streets where it belongs.'

Jacky turned toward him slowly. "You really got to understand something, Whitfield. We don't work for you.

You work for us. We supply the bimbos, you do what you're told."

"For God's sake, Jacky," Whitfield said. "I'm president of—"

"You're shit," Jacky said. "You work for us. Don't you?"

Whitfield stared at him. Jacky leaned slightly toward him.

"Don't you?"

Whitfield nodded slowly.

Jacky looked back at me. "You got any final words?" he said.

I said, "You know I've got all this stashed with someone so if I go down it goes to the cops."

"And if you don't go down?"

"Maybe it doesn't have to," I said.

"Nothing you can prove anyway."

"You know better, Jacky. The feds find out you're connected to this bank and they'll be all over you like leather on a baseball. They'll turn something up."

Jacky shrugged. "They've turned up stuff before. We're still in business."

"Sensible attitude," I said, "except you been acting just the other way, like if I got to Whitfield the sky would fall."

"So you got a proposition?" Jacky said.

"I want April Kyle, and I want to know what happened to Ginger Buckey."

"And that's all?"

I nodded.

"Okay," Jacky said, "take a hike. We'll get back to you."

I made a shooting gesture at Whitfield with my forefinger and thumb, and went on out. Downstairs in the lobby Hawk was leaning against one of the writing islands looking at two guys near the door.

He nodded toward them. "Mr. Milo?" he said.

"Un huh. Jacky was upstairs."

"I bet he mentioned shooting you," Hawk said. We were walking straight at the two guys near the door.

"Sort of. I offered him an alternative."

"He go for it?" Hawk said.

"We'll see," I said.

The two guys by the door moved aside as we reached them and we went out onto Franklin Street.

34

In the morning Jacky Wax came to see me. He came into my office wearing a three-piece blue suit and a pink tie and carrying a paper bag with two cups of coffee in it. He gave me a cup, and sat down in my client chair and opened the coffee, peeling the lid off away from himself so if any spilled it wouldn't get on his suit. I opened my coffee and had a swallow. Jacky had a little of his.

"Okay," Jacky said. "We are running a business, and we try to do what's best for the business. If it's best for business to kill somebody, we kill him. If it's best to buy somebody, we buy him, you unnerstand?"

"Un huh."

"If it's best to deal, we deal."

"Un huh."

"We want you to unnerstand that. Mr. Milo himself said he wanted that crystal clear, that you ain't getting away with something you shouldn't."

I nodded. Variety is the spice of life.

"So we like the deal," Jacky said.

"Which is?"

"Which is you get the bimbo back, and you leave everything else alone. Lehman, Whitfield. Everything else."

"Who takes the fall for Ginger Buckey?" I said.

"Who?"

"Ginger Buckey, the hooker got killed in New York. Somebody's got to go down for that."

"Why?"

"Christ, Jacky," I said, "I don't know. But somebody does. Nobody cared about her one day in her life."

"What fucking difference does it make to her now," Jacky said.

"I don't know that either, but somebody's got to pay the price. She's going to matter."

"You didn't say anything about this yesterday," Jacky said.

"I didn't know about this yesterday. Until just now I thought I was looking for April Kyle."

"And now you're not?"

"Her too, but we're going to get even for Ginger."

Jacky drank some more coffee. His long legs stretched out in front of him. His white shirt had French cuffs, I noticed. With sapphire cuff links. He swallowed a mouthful of coffee a little at a time and looked at me while he did it. He shook his head.

"You are a piece of fucking work," he said. "You know who you're dealing with. You've known it for a while. And you keep pushing anyway, and when you get lucky and we offer you a deal, you push more." Jacky shook his head.

"Kid's father was raping her when she was twelve. Then he sold her to a pimp, and he sold her to a pimp and so on and then somebody killed her."

"So her old man was a creep," Jacky said. "Don't matter anymore."

"I want somebody," I said. "Otherwise the whole thing goes down."

"You think you know what the whole thing is?" Jacky said.

"I know some, I guess some. I say Whitfield is washing money for you. I say he's got one of your dummy companies on an exempt list so that the cash transactions over ten grand don't get reported to the IRS. I say in return you have Perry Lehman supply him girls and a safe place to use them where his Boston Banker reputation doesn't get pecker tracks all over it. Maybe he gets a piece of what he washes, but I bet mostly it's women."

"And you figure we own Lehman?" Jacky said.

"Of course you do. He's operating high-class whorehouses all over the country. He never gets busted. Tony Marcus doesn't dare touch him. I annoy him and your guys appear."

"Makes sense," Jacky said.

"So I start looking for April Kyle, one day, and this is the part I don't get, and it trips some alarm someplace. I don't know why, but everybody starts panicking 'cause it's going to lead me to DePaul Federal. And somebody goes down to New York and starts closing doors."

"Sounds pretty fancy stuff for a simple laundry scheme," Jacky said.

"Scheme was simple enough, but it was worth saving. DePaul is the eighteenth biggest bank in the country," I said. "I looked it up. You run one of the biggest cash businesses in the country. Whitfield solves a lot of problems for you."

Jacky nodded and finished his coffee and looked around for the wastebasket.

"It's back here," I said. "Give it to me."

Jacky handed me the cup and I dropped it in the wastebasket.

"Whitfield likes young women," Jacky said. "And he likes a lot of things that women don't. So we supply him broads that don't have much choice. Ginger Buckey was one, but she took off on him with the coon, and she had to be replaced."

"And April was her replacement."

Jacky nodded. "We took her from the pimp who took the other whore away from Whitfield," Jacky said. "Whitfield liked that."

"And I came looking for her and in the process found Ginger for you."

Jacky nodded again. He was smiling faintly.

"And you didn't kill her to keep me from finding out about Whitfield. You killed her as an object lesson for April, or anyone else you might give Whitfield."

"Both," Jacky said. "We killed her for both reasons. We had the pimp do it."

"Rambeaux?"

"Yeah."

"And you beat him up for taking Ginger from Whitfield."

Jacky smiled wider. "Both," he said. "Teach him a lesson and make sure he don't say anything to you."

"And then when I kept at it you aced him to be sure."

"Yep. Been smarter to have aced you, way back at the beginning." Jacky stretched his neck as he talked, as if to loosen a kink in the right side. "But that's Monday morning. We decided to stay away from you if we could. People say you're hard to kill and you got friends that cause trouble. Bad for business. So we went the other way."

"Nobody's perfect," I said.

"So we already gave you somebody for Ginger Buckey. We gave you the guy that did her."

"Doesn't seem enough," I said.

"Better be," Jacky said. "That's all there is. Anything else would be bad business."

"You can't spare Lehman and you can't spare Whitfield," I said.

"That's right."

"Lehman thinks you tried to hit him," I said.

"I know."

"He's going to crack on you someday, Jacky."

Jacky shook his head. "You underestimate how scared he is," he said.

"Maybe," I said.

"You want the girl or not?" Jacky said.

"Yes," I said.

"We'll bring her here at noon. Keep something in mind, though. If anyone blows the whistle on Whitfield, there's no point to us not killing you then. Her too."

"I've thought of that," I said.

35

April Kyle showed up at noon. By herself. Carrying a small overnight bag. She wasn't dressed for work today. She had on jeans and a T-shirt and pale lemon jazz shoes. The T-shirt had a picture of a penguin on the front and the legend PENGUIN LUST underneath it. Her face was without makeup. She wore no lipstick. Her hair was pulled back in a ponytail and held partly in place by a pale yellow headband that matched her shoes.

She opened my office door and walked into the room and stopped in front of my desk and stood without moving, her head down, holding the overnight bag by the strap with both hands in front of her. She didn't speak. No one came in behind her.

"Long time no see," I said.

She nodded without looking up.

She hadn't closed the door when she came in and the corridor behind her remained empty. I got up and walked around my desk and out through the open door and looked up and down the corridor. No one was there. I closed the door and went back around the desk and sat down. April stood as she had, her eyes fixed on something near her feet.

"You okay?" I said.

She nodded again without looking up.

Maybe I should try to think of a question without a nod-shake answer.

"What would you like to do now?" I said. A master of sparkling small talk.

She shook her head.

"Had lunch?" I said.

She shook her head.

I could feel the first trickle of sweat in the small of my back.

"Well," I said, smiling warmly, "when in doubt, eat."

Normally my warm smile does it. Women often undress when I've given them my warm smile. April had no reaction at all. Probably because she didn't see it because she was still eyeing the floor. I thought of other approaches. *Look at me or I'll kill you?* Probably too direct.

I said, "Was it—" caught myself and rephrased. "How bad was it?" I said.

She didn't say anything. She kept her eyes down and shook her head again.

I got up and walked around the desk. I stood close to her without touching her.

"It won't be bad anymore," I said.

She nodded.

"You're with me," I said. "You're safe."

Nothing. Not even a nod.

"We have known each other for four years," I said. "I don't know if we ever actually liked each other, but we've known each other long enough to start."

More nothing.

"You want to see your parents?" I said.

She shook her head.

"You want to see Mrs. Silverman?"

Shrug. Shrug? Christ, a shrug was eloquent. I was on a roll.

"Okay, this evening we'll see Mrs. Silverman. You staying anyplace?"

She shook her head.

"Okay," I said. "You can stay with me."

She nodded.

"As a guest," I said, "your own room. No professional responsibilities."

She shrugged. The little chatterbox.

"Are there clothes or anything we should pick up?"

She shook her head.

"That's it? One overnight bag?"

She nodded.

"Okay," I said. "Then we'll go have a little lunch, maybe take a walk along the river and plan our next step."

She made no movement.

"There is a next step, kiddo," I said.

Her shoulders hunched slightly.

"And we'll plan it together."

Her shoulders hunched more and began to shake. Her breath came shorter and shorter and she was crying. I put my hands on her shoulders. She shrank in toward herself and pulled away without moving. I left my hands on her shoulders.

"You're all right now," I said. "You're with me, and you can stay with me as long as you want to."

The sobbing got louder and faster. I patted her shoulders where my hands rested.

"It won't happen to you again," I said. "Whatever it was, it won't happen again. I won't let it happen again."

She leaned her head forward against my chest and cried some more. I patted her shoulder some more. Then she suddenly lunged against me and pressed against me as hard as she could and put both arms around me and hugged as hard as she could. I shifted my hands from her shoulders and put my arms around her and held her firmly against me. She shook hard, her teeth chattering as she cried and her crying muffled as she pressed her face to my chest.

We stood that way for maybe ten minutes until the crying started to subside. It seemed more as if she wore out than as if she got control. Finally we were still, standing pressed together awkwardly, with the overnight bag clumsily on the floor between our feet. We stood maybe three or four more minutes like that, in perfect silence. Then she leaned slightly back from me without letting go and took a breath. And another and slowly her breathing began to regulate. She looked up at me for the first time. Her eyes were swollen and her nose ran.

"I'm sorry," she said. Her arms were still around me. Mine were lightly around her.

I nodded. "If you didn't want lunch," I said, "a simple no would have sufficed."

She made her lips smile, but it was simple politeness. Nothing seemed funny to her yet.

"There's a washbasin in the bathroom there," I said. "Go in and wash your face. Cold water is good. Then we'll consider lunch again."

"And then a walk," she said, "along the river?"

"Un huh."

"And . . ."

I shook my head. "We've planned far enough ahead. One step at a time, cookie."

She nodded and went in the bathroom. The water ran and I heard her splashing it on her face.

So far so good.